I0723178

# FALLING LESSONS

## STACEY ELZA

AURORA CORIALIS PUBLISHING

WWW.AURORACORIALISPUBLISHING.COM

**FALLING LESSONS**

COPYRIGHT © 2023 BY STACEY ELZA

All rights reserved. No part of this book may be used, reproduced, stored in a retrieval system, or transmitted by any means—electronic, mechanical, photocopy, microfilm, recording, or otherwise—without written permission from the publisher, except in the case of brief quotations embodied in critical articles or reviews.

This is a work of fiction. Names, characters, businesses, places, events, locales, and incidents are either the products of the author's imagination or used in a fictitious manner. Any resemblance to actual persons, living or dead, or actual events is purely coincidental.

For more information, address the publisher at cori@coriwamsley.com

Paperback ISBN: 978-1-958481-84-4

Ebook ISBN: 978-1-958481-85-1

Printed in the United States of America

Cover illustration and design by Karen Captline, BetterBe Creative

Edited by Renée Picard, Aurora Corialis Publishing

# PRAISE FOR FALLING LESSONS

"*Falling Lessons* is wonderful from the very first sentence. It reminded me of *Bridge to Terabithia*, *Seventeenth Summer*, and several Laurie Halse Anderson novels, all of which I personally count as setting a gold standard for YA fiction.

"The protagonist and narrator of *Falling Lessons*, Louisa, is not just a teenage girl whose life has suddenly been turned upside-down. She's also smart, funny, self-aware, and possessed of a dazzling—and sometimes uncomfortable—capacity for experiencing the world around her with her whole body. Her story is about fish, frogs, hapkido, and hurricanes. It's also about hanging on and letting go, falling in love and letting yourself be loved back. And because it's told in Louisa's remarkable voice, it's a story that offers unexpected moments of wonder on every page and reminds you to find and savor such moments in your own life."

—Ann Claycomb, *Silenced* and *The Mermaid's Daughter*

—

"Stacey Elza's *Falling Lessons* takes readers on a wild ride into the future—when the world as we know it seems quaint and technological advancement rules the day. Louisa, new to town and trying to fit in even with Tourette's, must traverse a sick grandmother, a burgeoning crush, and a boyfriend left behind as she tries to build a new life for herself. Elza manages to create a sense of nostalgia for our current world and an excitement for what's to come."

—Laura Leigh Morris, *Jaws of Life*

—

"Gentle, honest, and vulnerable, *Falling Lessons* is a compelling futuristic coming-of-age story about Louisa, a teenage girl facing the challenges of family, love, technology, and growing up."

—A.K. Downing, *The Air Series*, akdowning.com

—

"It was interesting to see the future through the eyes of Louisa, who battles life's obstacles beyond her control. Seeing her use the martial art of hapkido to turn those obstacles into opportunities shows how someone can overcome negativity by seeking positivity around them and by always looking for the good in themselves and others."

—Master Laura Beluschak, 7th Degree Black Belt, Hapkido

—

"*Falling Lessons* by Stacey Elza is a coming-of-age story that instantly brought me in from the first page. Although set in the future, the dialogue is carefully crafted and will take the reader back to a time of their innocent, honest, funny, and most intimate thoughts.

"Leaving you feeling as if you're a part of the conversations and events, this book reveals questions and answers about love and life. Whether familial moments that many of us will experience and the emotions that go with them, or love and the rollercoaster of emotions that come along for the ride, each interaction between the characters in *Falling Lessons* is real and deeply felt. Bringing a wonderful mix of nostalgia and reality for older readers and a sense of normalcy and excitement to the younger, *Falling Lessons* is a must-read for those who want to feel like they are right there in the action."

—Jess Branas, Founder/CEO of Branas Enterprises, Podcast Host of Drinks with Jess, Author of *Seeking Her, Knowing You* and *Zero to Ninety*

# TABLE OF CONTENTS

# CHAPTER 1

If I'd just taken Callisto with me, maybe she wouldn't be dead.

But how do you take a goldfish with you when a hurricane is headed your way? Do you fill a plastic bag with water and put her in there, like some carnival prize? Or do you use a cooler? Or do you use your mom's dough-rising bowl even though it's 40 years old and made of black walnut and what am I even talking about? That wooden bowl would leak all over the car, and the fish would die anyway, and Mom would yank the bowl out of my lap and beat me to death with it because that's her good bowl, dang it, and it's an antique.

I guess it doesn't matter now. Callisto's eyes look chalk-dust covered. They're just white. Deleted. And I'm standing in the yard—where the lawn chairs used to be before they blew away—and I'm holding her in my gloved hand. And my mom, my boyfriend Ezra, and his mama are all staring at me, waiting for me to do something.

Except I don't do anything. I just stand there like an idiot, taking deep, whooshy breaths while my respirator hangs loose around my neck. Because even though the air is as hot and heavy as potato soup out here, it's *still* better than the moldy air inside our house, where we were cleaning stuff out.

Finally, Mom breaks a stick off of one of the bazillions of branches on the ground. She uses it to start digging a hole in the dirt. "The least we can do is bury Callisto," she says. "I mean, you've had her since third grade, so what is that anyway? Five years?" She wipes the sweat and dirt off her face with the back of her hand. "We can do *one* thing right—give her a good sendoff—on this day when everything else is wrong."

I get an idea.

I set Callisto in the grass, grab Ezra by the shoulder, and pull him to our car, where everything we could salvage is packed up. I take a box labeled "HALLOWEEN" out of the back seat, but it's heavier than I think it'll be, and I drop it in the driveway. A robot witch cackles inside.

Ezra hitches his thumbs under his suspenders and laughs. "Looks like Hurricane Louisa's a category five. Expect a lot of property damage."

"Not funny," I say.

"Board up your windows. Bring your garbage cans inside."

"Quit it."

It's weird to have the same name as the storm that destroyed part of your county. And the next county over. And, OK, a lot of Florida. Why couldn't they have named it Hurricane Lola or Hurricane Leprechaun or Hurricane Lasagna or Hurricane Literally Anything Else?

I pull a trash bag stuffed with clothes out of the car. A GIF of a storm tearing off somebody's garage door slides onto my glasses, and I almost duck when the roof comes flying at me. Then there's a GIF of palm trees thrashing around me in the wind. I wave my hand in front of my face to clear my lenses. Sometimes I wish we still had phones like they did in the old days. That way, if somebody sent you a GIF, it couldn't jump-scare you so badly. It wouldn't be an inch from your face.

"Quit it," I say. "I'm serious."

Ezra's like, "OK, OK, fine. What are you up to anyway?"

"You'll see."

While I move a pile of shirts—still on their hangers—out of the way, I want to tell Ezra so many things: "I can't believe I'm moving to Palma Linda." "I can't believe I'm moving to Palma Linda *to live with my grandma.*" "Who's going to eat the red and yellow Starbursts and let me have all the pink and orange ones when you're not around? It's not even like Lilith and Dora will be there to do it. I won't have any friends in Palma Linda at all."

But what I actually say is, "Do you think fish fart?"

"Do I think fish fart?"

"Yeah."

"Do I think *fish fart?*"

"Yeah, I mean, they eat, right? And they probably have those good bacteria in their gut to help them break down their food—like the kind of bacteria in those capsules my mom takes. And those bacteria probably make gas, just like they do in us and dogs and cows and ... oh! Do you think insects fart?"

Ezra says I have a strange mind. I can't tell if that's a good thing or a bad thing.

He starts talking about these new paint pens he got, and how they're full of acrylic paint that's really vibrant—"like automotive paint," he says—and how there are 102 pens in this set. He says 250 bucks seemed like a lot to spend on pens, at first, but then he realized that if he wanted to make serious art, he needed to have serious tools. So, that's what he told his moms, and really, how could they argue with that?

"They couldn't," I say. And I wonder if there are other things he wants to say to me but can't: he'll miss me; he can't imagine going to school without me; he doesn't have the faintest idea who will eat the pink and orange Starburst now. But I know I can't ask him about any of *those* things, so I say, "Wait. A hundred and two pens? That's a weird number. Are the hundred-and-first pen and the hundred-and-second pen the only metallic ones in the set or—Oh! Hey, here it is, I found it!"

I pull out the bin marked "COMICS," open it, and start sifting through the comic books inside. These are my favorites, the ones I slipped into silicone sleeves and put on the top shelf of my closet before we evacuated ahead of the storm. The rest of them—on my short bookshelves—wilted in the rain that came through the roof.

"What are you doing with those?" Ezra asks, nodding toward the comics.

"I told you: you'll see."

"You should give them to me," he says, joking but also *not* joking. "Your grandma probably won't have room for them all in her little mobile home, and she'll make you throw them away. I can do you a favor and take them off your hands right now."

He picks up volume one of *Saturn Girl*, but I laugh, smack him on the arm, and take it back. "Nice try."

"Ezra!" his mama yells. "Hey, Ezra!"

We ignore her because it's just his mama. She'll call him two or three times before she gets good and mad, and even then, she won't punish him or anything. She'll just gripe a little. But if it was his *mom*, he'd have to fly over to her—and I do mean *fly*—because unlike his mama, his mom acts like a drill sergeant. *She* will ground him or suspend his data line or something if he ignores her even one time, which is totally unfair if you ask me. "Grandma won't make me get rid of my comics," I say, searching for a specific comic in the bin. "She's too nice for that. And besides: she's had all these, like, strokes? So, her memory's kind of bad. Well, it's worse than 'kind of' bad. That's like saying your mom is *kind of* strict, or the hurricane was *kind of* a bad storm, or a Toblerone is *kind of* a big candy bar. She has dementia, so she might forget I have any comics at—"

"*Ezra!* Hey. Get over here."

"—any comics at all. In fact, Mom keeps saying the hurricane might have been a 'blessing in disguise'"—I roll my eyes and make quotation marks in the air—"because now we get to look after Grandma and make sure she takes her meds and goes to her doctor's appointments and does what-all-ever else, I don't even *know*. Because she has good days, sure, but she also has bad—"

"*Ezra James Macy-Lane, don't make me count to three.*"

Then Ezra is kissing me, and it's hard to breathe because his nose is squashing my one working nostril and making my clip-on nose ring dig into my skin, but, like, I don't even mind because *it's happening*: I'm finally being kissed. We've officially been boyfriend and girlfriend for 35 days, and *it's finally happening, people!* He pulls away and looks me straight in the eyes. I feel hollow and squirmy, like a cave full of bats.

His mama yells, "One!"

"It's going to be OK," he tells me.

"Two!"

"You're, like, my girl, right?" Then he stuffs his hands in his pockets, yells, "All right, all right, I'm coming! Geez!" and squelches through the mud to his mama.

I turn to the box of comics.

*I'm, like, his girl, right?*

I find what I'm looking for: issue three of the *Mera* relaunch, the one with the black-and-white variant cover. I hug it to my chest and run back to the spot where Mom was digging the hole. Only now Ezra is digging it, and his mama is getting onto him for not digging it in the first place.

*I'm, like, his girl, right?*

I flip through the pages of *Mera* and rip out the one I'm looking for—the one that shows Mera fighting her arch nemesis on Neptune.

"OK," I say, "the thing is, Neptune is the god of the sea, right? And this scene takes place on Neptune, right?" I rip out the page and hold it up so Mom can see it. "It just seems—I don't know—appropriate that we send Callisto off with the god of the sea. So, I'm going to wrap her up in this picture. It's ... it's kind of corny, I know, but—"

"No," Mom says, "it's not corny at all. It's—"

"—but Callisto was, like, my friend, you know? And I don't want to just put her in the ground. I mean, I know I *am* putting her in the ground, obviously, but I don't want to put her in the *groundy* ground—"

Mom touches my shoulder. "Louisa. Hey. It's not corny, all right? It's not corny at all. It's nice."

My throat feels suddenly tight, and if I exhale, I'll cry, but I don't *want* to cry, so I hold my breath while I fold the page around Callisto. Then I clear my throat and start talking about something else—anything else. "OK, so basically, Mera is the queen of Xebel. And Xebel is—I don't know—space Atlantis. I saw an interview with the illustrator once. She said she based Xebel on 'what if you could live in the abandoned parts of Miami that are underwater?' So: seaweed wrapped around beach umbrellas, cars covered in algae, manatees swimming through hotel windows, that kind of thing."

Mom fans herself with the collar of her shirt. "It all sounds very interesting," she says, and I can't tell if she means it really *does* sound very interesting or if she's just saying that to make me feel better. I want to stop talking, but if I stop talking, I'll cry, so I keep babbling.

"The villain Mera is fighting on Neptune is named Black Manta. She traveled there from Xebel to battle him because he's, like, her nemesis? And, oh, also, listen to this: they're fighting while it rains diamonds. Because did you know it rains diamonds on Neptune—like, for real?"

By now, Ezra has finished digging the hole, so I put Callisto in it and cover her up. Then we all stare at the stew-like mud that's on top of her, and now I *do* cry, but just a tiny bit because I hold the rest of the crying in. The only sound besides my sniffling is a motorcycle growling down the street, behind a row of houses that don't have much siding left anymore.

Mom asks me if I have any words of remembrance to say for Callisto, but I can't think of a single thing to say. Not one thing. Which is terrible, really. Because I loved Callisto; no, I *love* Callisto. And because I talked to her practically every day: about getting 100 on a math quiz, about having my braces tightened, about lending somebody a comic and not getting it back. So, you'd think I'd be able to talk to her now. And there's a good chance one night, at two in the morning, I'm going to wake up for no good reason, and I'm going to have tons of ideas about what to say. But right now I just say, "Uh, goodbye?"

"Farewell, Callisto," Mom says. "You were a good pet and an even better friend. You will be missed. May Lord Neptune welcome you into his watery bosom."

"*Mo*-om!"

Then, before I know it, she's hugging Ezra and his mama, and thanking them for all their help, and calling them angels, and saying, "Now, if y'all need anything—I mean *anything*—just text me, day or night, OK? I mean it. Day or night. And when we get settled, here's what I'm going to do: I'm going to bake you a double batch of gingersnaps and send them to wherever you're staying." She looks at Ezra's mama. "I know they're your favorite. No, no, you can't talk me out of it. My mind is made up."

She puts her arm around my shoulders and squeezes me tight against her, which I don't think she's done since I was six years old and tried to sit on the back of our porch swing, and the swing flipped, and I ripped that little piece of skin that connects your gums to the inside of your upper lip, and there was blood everywhere.

She says, "Well, Louisa?" Her voice breaks. She clears her throat. "Guess we'd better get on the road." She dims the lenses of her glasses as dark as they'll go. That means she's about to cry and wants us all to pretend she isn't—which, I mean, honestly? I don't like it when people catch me crying either. I'd rather they caught me picking my nose or having a whole conversation with a goldfish or un-ironically watching the *Backyard-again-igans*.

Ezra and I lock eyes. I wonder if he'll kiss me one more time. Or if I'll kiss him. Or if he'll ask if I want help putting the stuff back in the trunk, and oh my God, I forgot to put the stuff back in the trunk, and Mom's going to kill me when she finds out. But he just looks at his mama and back at me real quick, and he says, "So. Bye, Louisa. I ... bye."

He doesn't kiss me. He doesn't even hug me. He waves.

And I get it. Like, really: I get it. His mama's looking at us. *My* mom's looking at us. I bet he feels as awkward as I did when I couldn't think of anything to say for Callisto besides goodbye.

So I wave back. "Bye."

Then Mom and I walk toward our car, which will drive us to a hotel that the wind and rain of the hurricane couldn't quite reach. In that hotel is a room that smells like when you carve a jack-o-lantern, and in that room is a jumble of bins and suitcases and trash bags, and in *those* is everything we took with us when we fled before the storm hit: our birth certificates; cricket bars and juice boxes; my Tourette's meds, which sometimes work; Mom's antidepressants, which never work; the cat clock with the eyes that go back and forth, even though that's totally random. Stuff like that. And that's it. That's all we have left to take with us when we check out of the hotel, keep driving north, and reach Grandma's house that's just south of the Alabama border. I don't even have my fish anymore.

I just have my favorite comics.

And I have "Bye."

# CHAPTER 2

Mom and I have been on the road for over an hour, trying to get from our hotel to Grandma's mobile home, but rain is kerplunking on the windshield, and the car is driving us at the speed of continental drift.

When we get to a red light, I climb to the back seat to get a comic book. That way I can read about Mera fighting Black Manta, or Black Canary fighting Vertigo, and pretend like none of this is happening. But Mom tells me to hurry up back there and sit down because the car won't move if I'm not buckled in.

"We're barely moving anyway," I say, "so what's the point?"

But she's like, "Sit!" So I grab some comics at random, sit back down, snap my seat belt, and stare at the purplish-blue flowers growing in the ditch, like I *didn't* just get a handful of comic books so I could avoid staring at ditch-flowers.

"I think that's chicory—those flowers, I mean," Mom says for no reason. "Chicory's the stuff they use in Coffake. That's what *I* heard, anyway. I also heard they're coming out with Coffake that has real coffee in it, too. Forty percent chicory, 60% coffee. I might even be able to get your grandma to drink *that*. She's always been picky, but she's been even pickier since ... well, since *you know*."

"You can say 'stroke,' Mom. It's not going to traumatize me."

Mom sighs and turns on a classic-pop station. It's playing Taylor Swift. It's always playing Taylor Swift. I'm pretty sure it's been playing Taylor Swift since before Taylor Swift was born.

"Remember how your grandma was when we saw her last Thanksgiving? A little bit forgetful but not majorly different? Well, I think she might be worse now. Like, her texts have been getting stranger. A couple weeks ago, she texted me to ask where her texting app went, but she was texting me *from her texting app*. I still don't know what that was all about. Another time, she texted me to ask where to buy urine remover, except she couldn't remember the word 'urine'–or the word 'remover'–so she kept saying she needed stuff to 'stop pee.' I thought it was some medical thing. I was grilling her about her blood sugar levels, freaking out and thinking her diabetes was making her pee too much. But, nope. She just needed urine-remover spray and couldn't remember that you can buy it online. Or at a pet store. Or at a grocery store. Or at literally any big-box store."

"Why would Grandma even need urine-remover spray? She doesn't have a cat. She doesn't have a dog. She just has an aquarium."

"I was afraid to ask." Mom turns up Taylor Swift.

I open an issue of *Black Canary* and hold it up so it's hiding my whole face. "Did you guys not know about many artists in the twenties, or what? Because these classic stations are always playing the same dozen songs."

Mom says the classic station doesn't play every song that came out back then, and there were plenty of artists that made deep, serious music, like *blah blah blah* ... I tune her out as I look at *Black Canary*. I'm in the middle of a fight scene—a series of panels where Black Canary lets out her ultrasonic canary cry to hurl a bunch of goat-headed monsters across the bowling alley—when the car slows to a stop. There's a branch blocking part of the road, and the car isn't smart enough to go around it, so Mom has to put her hands on the steering wheel and do it herself. Once she's past it, the car takes over again.

Mom mutters, "We can send people to Mars, but we can't build a car that recognizes a stick."

"We're never going to get to Grandma's."

"Just close your eyes. Take a nap."

"I'm not tired. It's one o'clock in the afternoon."

"Just close your eyes."

I turn a page in *Black Canary* so hard that I practically smack it. Now Black Canary is kicking a monster in the face, and the monster's spitting everywhere like *ptooey!* Now she's kicking another monster in the chest so hard that he sails down the bowling lane and knocks all the pins over, and she's like, "Strike!"

Mom says, "Suit yourself," and falls asleep before the Taylor Swift song ends.

# CHAPTER 3

The last time I saw Grandma in person, she was wearing a red dress with white, gingerbread-house-looking trim and black, patent-leather shoes with ankle straps. She was standing on her front deck, smiling and waving while we drove away, and the sun was setting, and I had to block it with my hand as I looked back at her. And the whole time we rode home, the care package she made us take with us was leaking gravy on the back seat. But we didn't find out until we got home, and when Mom saw it, she walked straight into the house without saying a word, sat on the floor in front of the fridge, and ate Crick-or-Treat ice cream straight out of the carton. When a blob of pumpkin-pie-flavored ice cream and chocolate-covered cricket fell on her jeans, she didn't even wipe it off.

This time, Grandma couldn't possibly wear those ankle straps even if she wanted to—even if they *wouldn't* look ridiculous with her orange cardigan and mango-print leggings. Her right foot and ankle are pink and swollen and shiny, like they're made of SPAM. It's got to be painful when she meets us at the car and walks barefoot over the crushed-seashell driveway.

After she hugs me, I'm like, "Is your foot OK?"

And Mom's like, "Yeah, that looks infected. Have you seen your doctor about it, or ... ?"

But Grandma says, *it doesn't hurt at all*, and *stop touching it, Bella, it doesn't feel warm, just leave it alone.* And *how did you get to be so tall? And how old are you now? Fourteen! How is that possible? It feels like you should still be playing with dolls.*

"Oh, she still has dolls," Mom says, nudging me. "Comic-book dolls."

"They're not dolls, Mom. They're *figurines.*"

"Well, let me welcome you and your figurines to"—Grandma switches to a game-show-host voice—"*your new home.*" She sweeps her arm in front of the mobile home, like *tah-dah!*

The first thing I notice about Grandma's deck—the first thing *anyone* would notice about Grandma's deck—is her collection of frogs. There's a ceramic frog playing a banjo and a ceramic frog vaping. There's a terracotta frog with a dead fern that *used* to be growing out of its head. Three plastic angel frogs are praying in a semicircle. One frog is completely covered in fake moss and has a pinecone bird feeder hanging from its hand ... or, its foot? I don't know what to call it. Another one is dressed like a chef cooking frog legs, which is just ... yeah.

I make myself sound like a shouty game show host, too, because I don't even *know* why. I guess I'm nervous. *"These decorative frogs add a touch of whimsy to your new redwood deck."*

*"And that's not all!"* Grandma says. *"You've also won ... a batch of splat."*

I wrinkle my nose. "What's splat?"

"Do you like Rice Krispies?"

"Yeah."

"Do you like cheese?"

"Um, yeah?"

"Then you'll like splat."

When we follow Grandma past all the frogs, I can hear yelling and gunshots coming from the other side of the front door before she even opens it. Once we're inside, I see what she was watching: a video-game play-through. A policeman is shooting a zombie—*pop, pop, pop*—and the zombie goes *aaargh!* and splashes into a swamp full of cypress trees and Spanish moss. I'm tempted to tell the TV to lower the volume, but I don't want to be rude.

Grandma hands me a tray of bumpy, yellow blobs. I'm not sure what she wants me to do with them. Are they all for me? Does she want me to set them down somewhere? I balance the tray on the arm of the couch, push a mound of laundry off one of the cushions, and sit down.

This is weird: Grandma's house was always cluttered before, but it was never messy. Now I can't even put the tray down on the coffee table, like a normal person, because it's covered in junk. Yeah, there's her usual stuff—an ancient first-gen Switch with a cracked screen; a porcelain tree you open and there's candy inside; a glass bell with the date of King William and Queen Catherine's coronation etched into it—but there's also straight-up trash: wadded-up cinnamon-gum wrappers, empty ketchup packets, dried-out French fries.

Grandma picks up a used tissue from the seat of her recliner before she sits down. She stuffs the tissue into her cardigan sleeve.

"Aren't you hot in that?" I ask.

"In what?"

"In *that*. It's 100 degrees out there, but you're sitting there in a sweater, looking like back-to-school shopping."

She shrugs. "Good thing we're not outside then."

"Yeah, but like, it's still hot in *here*, you know?"

"Well, I don't know what to tell you. I guess the older I get, the colder I get. Heh. That rhymes." She pulls the lever that makes her chair recline, and the footrest flies up with a *thunk*. "How old are you now anyway? Thirteen?"

"Fourteen." But I already told her that.

"*Fourteen.*"

I realize I'm staring at the bottom of her foot. There's a round sore at the base of her big toe. It looks like a red dot in the middle of a red ring: a googly eye you'd find on the face of a haunted puppet. Then I notice Grandma is staring at *me* staring at *her*, so I look at her fish tank real quick. It's next to her recliner—on a table with curlicue legs—surrounded by crumpled, yellow napkins and crushed Dr. Pepper cans. I'm thinking she must never clean the tank because the water's so hazy I can't even guess how many fish are in there. It looks like they're drifting through wildfire smoke.

She's got some live plants in there, too, and they're growing like *woah*. A huge clump of hornwort is floating at the surface and trailing all the way down to the gravel. The Amazon swords are so tall they've got to be pressing against the lid by now. The only thing I can figure is there's so much fish poop and decaying fish food and probably decaying *fish* in there that the plants are thriving in a compost heap. Somehow, Grandma has kept some fish alive in all that filth.

Not that I'm bitter or anything.

"They're pretty, aren't they?" Grandma makes *koochy-koochy-koo* fingers at the fish. "They're guppies. I tell you what, though: I buy fish, and they die. I buy more fish, and they die. I just can't figure it out. Why do they keep dying?"

Yeah, Grandma. Big mystery.

She points at the tank. "See?" I don't see. "There. Right there. That's another dead one. I can't believe it. Louisa, get me that net, will you? It should be down there somewhere."

There's a shelf under the aquarium, full of mail and cookie wrappers and more Dr. Pepper cans and—for some reason—a scrap of paper that has "Sun tea little squirrels" scrawled on it. There's also a tiny jar with two gray chunks floating in it.

I pick up the jar and ask Grandma what it is.

"My tonsils."

I put down the jar.

I knock one of the Dr. Pepper cans over. It's not totally empty, and I get old Dr. Pepper on my arm.

Grandma laughs. "Watch out for that storm surge, everybody! It's Hurricane Louisa!"

I roll my eyes. "Found it." I lift the aquarium lid to scoop out this dead fish, and the stench makes me gag. It smells like every time somebody throws up at school and the janitor mops it up. But, in a way, I'm glad for the smell because it distracts me from how much this task reminds me of all the times I cleaned out Callisto's tank.

Grandma says it must be time to head back to the pet store and get more fish—because apparently any fish is as good as any other to her? "*Oooh*! I know: this time I should get some goldfish. Maybe half a dozen. Y'all think they'd get along with the guppies? Would they give them a hard time?"

"They wouldn't give them a hard time," I say, "but the thing is, guppies and goldfish need different water temperatures. Your thermometer is reading 80 degrees right now." Or 88. It's hard to tell through the haze. "That's OK for tropical fish, like guppies. But goldfish aren't tropical. They prefer room-temperature water. And also? You don't want to overcrowd your tank."

Grandma stares at me.

"I used to have my own goldfish," I say. "You know, *before*. But then the storm happened, and ... well, I don't have one anymore." And, just like that, I start to remember a lot of other things I don't have anymore. All the memories arise at once. It's like when a printer's offline, but people keep sending jobs to it, and when it comes back online, it spits out everything at once, whether anybody wants it anymore or not.

I remember the rattly peacock that hung on my closet door. I'd had it ever since I was a baby, and I loved the noise it made whenever I opened or closed that door, so why didn't I take it with me when we evacuated? And why didn't I take Emma, my American Girl doll with the tiny mask and the even tinier bottle of hand sanitizer? Or the nose-and-mustache glasses Lilith gave me last year, the day after she realized she could do such a good impression of me that she could activate my Glazier? Or my music box with the ballerina inside that looks creepily like me—same long, brown hair; same pointy chin; same freckles; same asymmetrical eyebrows, even? Or the spelling-bee trophy I won last year? I mean, it's a spelling-bee trophy with a misspelling on it: "seventh grape" instead of "seventh grade." I could have handed that down as an heirloom one day! My kids and grandkids would have thought that was hilarious.

I force myself not to cry and ask Grandma what she wants me to do with the dead fish. Does she want to flush it or bury it or what?

She waves her hand at me, like *you're dismissed*, and says, "Oh, just flush it down the toilet."

"Like all your money," Mom mutters.

The mobile home is so small, and the walls are so thin, that even when I'm in the bathroom—with the fish net dripping on my foot—I can still hear Mom telling Grandma that any new fish she buys will probably just die anyway. She uses her fake-happy voice when she asks her, "Have you considered how much money you're spending on these fish that don't even live?" It's the same tone a waitress would use to say they're sorry, they can't take the mealworms out of your bug burger for you.

Grandma clicks her tongue. "Bella, you're such a worrywart. How much does a goldfish cost, anyway? Ten dollars? Twenty dollars?"

"You can't get goldfish, Grandma," I mumble to myself.

She goes on: "A goldfish can't cost much. And, anyway, it's not like I'm a child. I'm a grown woman—"

Mom says, "Nobody's saying you're a child."

"—and I can spend my money on whatever I want. In fact, you know what? Let's go to the pet store. Let's all go. I'll drive. Just let me get my keys." She puts her footrest back down.

Mom says, "Your bumper still has a dent in it from last week. You shouldn't—" I know she wants to say that Grandma shouldn't be driving anymore. "If you wait until tomorrow, I can take you in our Osiris. You'll love it. It's a 2049—the new model."

"I'm not riding in your car."

"I know you're scared of—"

*"I'm not riding in your car."*

"Autonomous cars are safer than human-driven ones."

"You can't make eye contact with a car."

I flush the fish, leave the net on the counter to dry, and go sit on the couch again. I get this—how to describe it?—*nervousness* in my arms. It's this feeling that I have to flail them in the air, like I'm riding a rollercoaster and going *wooo!* I try to ignore it, but the tic slips out anyway. I knock the tray of splat on the floor and start to pick it up. It's squishy, like the organs of a small mammal. I feel like I'm picking up chipmunk lungs or mouse hearts.

Grandma stops arguing with Mom long enough to tell me, "That's OK. They're already called *splat*. In fact, why don't you bring me one? A little dirt never hurt. Ha! That rhymes."

Mom walks over to Grandma and pushes the sleeve of her cardigan up. The tissue falls out.

Grandma has a daisy tattoo on her arm that shows whether her blood sugar level is healthy or not. Blue petals mean it's too low. Yellow petals mean it's too high. Green petals mean it's just right. I've been trying to convince Mom to let me get an anchor tattoo on my ankle. I've been telling her it's so I can keep track of when I'm getting dehydrated, but really I just think it would look cool.

Grandma swats her away. "What are you doing? Get off of me."

Mom tries again. "I just want to check your sugar before you eat that splat. We don't want it to spike."

"Get *off* of me."

"Have you checked your sugar today?"

"Of course."

"Oh, really? Then what was it?"

Grandma watches the policeman open a loot box on the TV. There's a bronze axe inside. Without looking at Mom, she says, "I checked it." Which means she didn't.

I try to change the subject: "Grandma, you can get something that works like your tattoo, only it's for your aquarium. It's this test kit where you take a water sample—"

"It's looking kind of yellow," Mom says, turning Grandma's arm at different angles so she can get a better look.

"*Pffft*. Does not. Louisa, come look at this. Tell your mom it's green."

I stuff some splat in my mouth so I don't have to answer. It tastes like earwax.

Mom picks up a yellow napkin and holds it up next to the tattoo. "See? Yellow."

"Well, yeah, if you put *that* next to it. Louisa, I'm serious, come look at this. Tell your mom this is green. Yellowish green."

I force myself to swallow the splat. I step over to Grandma and try not to think about the film of cheese—or quote-unquote "cheese"—that's still coating my tongue. "It's ... chartreuse?"

"See?" says Mom. "What'd I tell you?"

But Grandma's like, "What do you mean, 'See'? Chartreuse is green."

"No, it isn't. *OK, Glazier: What color is chartreuse?*" And I know Mom's glasses are showing her examples of chartreuse now: a grid of chartreuse paint samples and fabric swatches and leaves or butterflies or parakeets or whatever actually *is* chartreuse in the world. "A-ha!" she says. "See? *Yellow*." She sends the search results to my glasses. Chartreuse is the color of unripe bananas. The color of seasickness.

Grandma picks up her phone from under an empty potato chip bag (that's right, her *phone*; her glasses aren't smart) and does her own search. She smiles and hands her sticky phone to me. It's got the same search results on it. "That's as green as green can be."

I stare at the speech-bubble icon in the corner of my left lens until the texting app opens. I text Ezra, using my eyes to glance at the letters on the keyboard and letting autocomplete finish each word once my glasses have guessed it: "Call me. Nothing bad, just urgent."

When he does, I announce to Mom and Grandma that Ezra's calling me, and I should really, really take this because it's really, really important. I walk out onto the deck, let the screen door slam behind me, and whisper-scream while my glasses fog up in the humidity.

I'm catching him up on everything when he interrupts me: "Hey, what's that? That green thing to your left. No, your *other* left. Next to the deck chair."

"Oh, that? That's Cedric. Cedric is Grandma's favorite ceramic frog. I named him."

Ezra laughs. "Oh my God, but why does it look like the Buddha though?"

"Oh, please. Doesn't *everyone* have a frog statue that looks like the Buddha? I know I keep mine with my other sacrilegious statues—next to my Lord Vishnu octopus."

"Yeah? Well, I keep *mine* next to my ceramic elephant that looks like Ganesha."

"Ganesha *is* an elephant."

"What?"

"Ganesha. The Hindu god, *Ganesha*."

"Yeah."

"He's an elephant. We learned that in social studies."

"We *did*? No, we didn't."

"Yeah, like, a month ago. Remember? The day we had the bomb threat? And we all had to go outside and sit in the parking lot, and the cops showed up, and Dora got stung by that wasp?"

"Louisa, what are you talking about?"

"*Remember?* And when we finally went back inside, Mr. McNamara did world religions? And he started with Hinduism?"

"That bomb threat was last week."

"What?"

"The bomb threat? It was just last week."

"No. That's not possible. You've got to be wrong about that. You're wrong."

But even as I'm saying it, I realize it *is* possible, and he *isn't* wrong, and then neither of us talks for a minute because how can it be that less than a week ago, we were sitting in social studies, texting each other about the new *Mera* movie and ignoring the map of India on the screen? Does the screen still work, I wonder? Is it still on the wall at the front of the room, next to Mr. McNamara's desk? Or is it covered up with branches and splotches of mold?

I don't like to think too hard about all that, so I show Ezra the other frogs on Grandma's deck. "Behold!"

"Oh my God."

"There are 22 of them. I counted them last time I was here."

Ezra starts making fun of them. They're tacky, they're embarrassing. But you know what? I can't even hate them. "They're so ugly, they're cute," I say, "and not much is cute here in *Palma Linda*."

Of course, as soon as my glasses hear "*Palma Linda*"—the town Grandma lives in— they try to be helpful by translating it from Spanish to English. A tiny voice whispers, "Beautiful palm," in my right ear. But that's not helpful at all. That's like saying somebody moved to The Angels instead of Los Angeles.

I swear, I hate this translator. Either it's wrong, or it's whispering at you when you don't even care that some Bengali-speaking kid is begging his mom for a Slinky, and his mom is snapping at him like, "Can we eat this Slinky, Partho? Can we?" And it doesn't matter how many times I turn the translator off. Sooner or later, it turns itself back on. I'm always having to go to Settings and navigate through all these sub-menus to silence it again.

I dive into sub-menus while Ezra changes the subject. He asks if I want to see his new "cute bedroom," only he says it in a way that means it isn't cute at all.

Next thing I know, the white walls of his FEMA trailer are filling my lenses. He's giving me a tour. No one could call this trailer a mobile home. It's practically an RV. The window blinds are white. The fridge is white. The fold-out couch that's his bed now is white. Just about the only things that aren't white are the dark-blue comforter and pillow on the couch. I recognize them from his old bedroom. I wonder if the pillow still smells like his pomade: citrusy and sunny. It was such a hopeful smell—the smell of buying raffle tickets or ordering appetizers or seeing the lights dim before a movie starts—and the thought of it makes me sad, but it's, like, a *happy* sad.

I point out how white everything is in his trailer. He tells me it's like living inside a milk carton.

Something about that makes me think of cartons of ice cream, and then ice cream sandwiches. "Hey," I say, "do you ever … ? No, never mind, forget it."

"Do I ever what?"

"Don't worry about it. It's weird."

"Well, now I *have* to know."

If I'm talking, I'm not thinking about the smell of his pomade and how much I miss it, so I explain: "Do you ever feel like different numbers smell like different things? I don't mean you write down the number *3*, and you scratch and sniff it like a sticker, and you smell ice cream sandwiches. I mean you write down the number three—or you see it on a football uniform or in the trailer for *Mera 3*—and your *imagination* smells ice cream sandwiches. It's like how, when you get a song stuck in your head, you don't hear it in your actual ears. Only instead of a song you don't hear in your ears, it's a scent you don't smell in your nose."

"You're right," Ezra says. "That *is* weird."

"You asked!"

"No, no, it's cool. I mean, it's cool but also ... atypical?"

"That's it," I grouch, joking–not joking. "I'm never telling you anything ever again."

"No, no, I want to know! You're like a dog. Only, no, not like that. I mean it in a good way. You smell more than you see. What does a three really smell like anyway? *Does* your imagination think it smells like ice cream sandwiches? Does every number have a smell?"

I barely get done telling him that a nine smells like Play-Doh when a text from Mom pings up on my glasses, right across Ezra's chin: "Come here."

I close the text. I ask Ezra, "And remember the time your mama put that metal comb on the stove and tried to straighten her hair with it?"

"Yeah." He chuckles. "That was amazing."

"Remember that smell? That's what a number one smells like. And a two smells like fried food—"

"We're going to the pet store," Mom texts. Then: sighing emoji.

"I've got to go. I'll call you back later, OK?"

"OK."

"I mean it. I'll call you after dinner. I'll tell you about the other number smells, OK?"

"OK."

"I love you." It's out of my mouth before I realize what's happening.

"OK," Ezra says.

Pause.

Oh, God.

Pause.

What have I done?

But then Ezra says, "Just kidding," and laughs. "I love you, too."

"I hate you."

"No, you don't. You love me. You just said so."

"Oh, hush." Mom texts a mad emoji. "OK, for real now, I've got to go."

The call ends. My lenses clear. I whisper to Cedric, "He loves me." I whisper to the cannibal-chef frog, "He loves me." And when Mom flings the screen door open and stomps to the car in the driveway, I whisper to her—once she's too far away to hear—"He loves me." Then I say, louder: "What are you doing?"

She opens the rear passenger door. "It's worse than I thought."

"What is?"

"She's got to go to the pet store *right now*. God forbid we wait a day." Mom gets an armful of cookbooks. One of them tumbles onto the driveway. I pick it up: *Entertaining with Entomophagy*. There's a platter of chocolate-covered grasshoppers on the cover. "If I don't take her, Lord knows she might drive herself, and then she'd be putting herself in danger. And other people, too."

I pick up more of Mom's cookbooks for her: *Basic Brunch*, *Harvest Home*, *Mind Your Biscuits*, and something just called *Pie*. I ask Mom again, "What's worse than you thought?"

"Your grandma. Her thinking. Her judgment. Her—oh, you know—her *demeanor*."

"So, she wants some more fish. So what?"

Mom sighs. "Part of her dementia is not understanding how much the dementia affects her. She doesn't think it's affected her at all. I've told her, and her doctor's told her, and probably Siri has told her—"

"Wait. Who's Siri?"

"—but no, according to your grandma, it's all some *huge conspiracy*. Either that, or the doctors are idiots. It's always one or the other with her. 'These Gen Alpha doctors just want to kill all of us Millennials off already. 'These Gen Beta doctors don't know how to *know* anymore. They just ask the AI everything. The AI could say I have prostate cancer, and the doctors would believe it."

"Mom. *Mom.* What's the big deal? It's just fish."

Mom doesn't answer. She just starts to cry. Or laugh. It's hard to tell which. But then she puts her glasses into sunglasses mode, which means she's crying.

She sniffles. "If we get out of that pet store without paying 100 bucks or more, I'll let you get that tattoo you want."

"Are you ... are you serious?"

She wipes her nose on her sleeve. "I don't even know anymore."

# CHAPTER 4

Grandma slides her swollen foot out of her glittery flip-flop and props it on the dash. She gestures to a road we've already flown past. "Hey, isn't that the way to the pet store?"

Mom tells her no. The car knows where to go. She points to the control panel. "See? This blue dot is us. And if I zoom out, you can see this green dot. That's the pet store."

"We should have turned right, way back there, where the gun-and-ice-cream store used to be."

Mom turns up the classic-pop station. It's that song where every other word in the chorus is "thunder." She drums along on the steering wheel and puts her lenses further into sunglasses mode. "I have no idea where the gun-and-ice-cream store used to be."

"I'm telling you where it used to be: it used to be back there. Look, just tell the car to make a U-turn, up here at the light, and go back." And before Mom even has a chance to tell the car anything, Grandma's like, "*OK, Osiris: turn around.*"

"Grandma, that's not how it—"

"*Hey, Osiris: turn around. Hey. Osiris. Turn. Around.*" She taps something on the control panel. The music gets louder. *THUNDER! TH-TH-THUNDER!*

Mom tells her to stop touching things.

She doesn't.

A message on the console says the child safety locks are now engaged.

Then a forecast is blaring: "MORE OF THE SAME TOMORROW, WITH PARTLY CLOUDY SKIES. HIGHS IN THE UPPER 90."

Grandma yells and slaps the armrest with every word: "Hey! Car! Turn! Around!"

"HEAT INDEX WILL REACH 105 IN SOME PARTS OF THE STATE. STAY INDOORS IF YOU CAN."

Grandma taps the console again. The car goes into manual mode and drifts off the road. The tires crunch on the gravel, and I'm like, this is it: I'm going to die. I'm going to die listening to the weather report and staring at my grandma's SPAM foot.

But Mom guides the car back onto the road. The crunching stops. My chest feels tight, like somebody just walked by wearing too much cologne. Mom lets out a long, slow, blowing-out-birthday-candles breath and turns off the radio. The forecast stops mid-sentence: "LOOK OUT FOR RAIN LATER THIS—"

No one says a word until the car is parking in front of Mill Creek Plaza, and Grandma says, "Y'all know this used to be a real mall, right?" in this totally normal voice like she *didn't* almost just kill us. "I remember. A *mall*-mall. It had a Sears where the nursing home is now and a B. Dalton where they sell those edible grasshoppers." She makes an *ick* face.

"Oh!" I say. "Do they have chili-lime? Because I could go for some chili-lime grasshoppers right about now. With tamarind sauce." My mouth starts to water.

"That's nasty." She changes the subject. "Louisa, do you know what B. Dalton even *was*?" She doesn't wait for me to answer. "B. Dalton was a bookstore. It sold actual books.

*Book*-books. Hey, Bella, my door's locked. I can't get out. *OK, Osiris: unlock my door.* Oh! It worked."

"No, Mom," she says. "That was me."

As we walk across the parking lot, I fan my glasses with my hands to try to stop them from fogging up. Ads from Mill Creek Plaza start to fill my lenses: an orthodontist who will PRINT YOUR BRACES WHILE YOU WAIT; a biometric opal that tracks your periods; a random accordion; 10 lessons for $99.95 at the Cypress Grove Hapkido Studio, whatever that is; buy-two-get-one-free hamsters; a pack of 102 paint pens just like the ones Ezra bought last week.

"Maybe it wasn't a B. Dalton," Grandma says. "Maybe it was a Waldenbooks."

Mom tells her it doesn't matter if it was a B. Dalton or a Waldenbooks.

And Grandma's like, "No. No, I remember now. It was definitely a B. Dalton. Definitely. Louisa, listen to this: you'll never guess what they sold out of the back room of the B. Dalton." She waggles her eyebrows at me.

"OK, that's enough for now," Mom says.

"I never saw it myself, of course, but everybody *said* they sold—"

"*Mom!* Enough!"

Grandma gives Mom's shoulder a little push. "I never would have taken you for a prude. Louisa's old enough to hear these things. How old are you again, anyway? 12?"

"I'm 14."

"*Fourteen!* I can't believe it. You should still be playing with baby dolls. Bella, shouldn't she still be playing with baby dolls?"

Before Grandma can bring up B. Dalton again, Mom asks me if I saw that hapkido ad on my glasses, too.

"Yeah. I mean, it showed up on my lenses, but I didn't actually *watch* it." Because obviously.

"You should watch it. It looks like fun."

"OK, so by saying that, you're guaranteeing it's not fun at all."

"There's exercise and meditation—"

"Wow. So fun."

"—and I think it could be good for your tics. Glazier showed me an article about it the other day."

"Oh, boy. Amazing."

"And your neurologist said that exercise can make your tics less severe. *And* your therapist is all about meditation. You should at least watch the video."

I cross my arms. "I thought we were here to buy fish."

"Bruh, you should watch it."

"Stop saying 'bruh.' It makes you sound like you're old enough to live in that nursing home that used to be a Sires."

"Sears," Grandma corrects me.

"*Just watch it!*" Mom snaps.

"Fine." I glare at the hapkido ad to activate the video. People in karate uniforms are kicking at their reflections in a mirror. Only, wait: I guess they're actually hapkido uniforms? Now some of the people are tumbling on the ground. Now an old lady in a hapkido uniform is meditating. Now water is trickling from the beak of a fountain shaped like a crane. Words appear: "Cypress Grove Hapkido Studio. Focus. Friendship. Respect." When the ad is over, it shrinks to the corner of my right lens—a tiny thumbnail.

Mom's staring at me like *well?*

I just say, "Why couldn't the third word start with an *f*, too?"

"What are you talking about?"

"In the ad: 'Focus. Friendship. Respect.' Like, why not make it 'Focus. Friendship. Faith.' Or 'Focus. Friendship. Fitness.' There. That's better."

"*That's* what you took from the ad?"

"Yes."

"The fact that you don't like their wording."

"Yes."

Mom sighs. "Now, look." And I know whatever she says next is going to be bad. Because nobody ever said, "Now, look," before something good. Like, "Now, look. Here's a bunny." Or, "Now, look. I booked an underwater hotel suite in the Sea of Cortez." Or, "Now, look. I made you an appointment with the tattoo artist, and now that you're 14, you're old enough for a tasteful anchor tattoo on your ankle, and I was wrong when I said you weren't." I mean, just for example. "We're going to stop by this hapkido place after the pet store. We'll just check it out. It won't take long."

"But I don't want to do hapkido."

"We're just checking it out."

"I don't *want* to do hapkido."

"How can you know for sure until you've checked it out?"

"Let's take *you* to check out alligator wrestling, Mom. Because how can you know for sure you don't want to wrestle alligators until you've checked it out?"

Grandma snickers. Mom glances at her like *zip it*. "I'll rephrase: we're checking out the hapkido studio to see if *I* might want you to do it."

I walk faster to get away from both of them. "I'm not going." I shove Mill Creek Plaza's main door open as hard as I can. "I refuse."

Before the door has even closed behind me, yellow arrows—the same shade as Grandma's high-blood-sugar daisy petals—appear on the floor, pointing me toward deep-fried grasshoppers with a small coke, 20%-off cookies, and that opal again. While Mom and Grandma catch up to me, I ask Glazier where the pet store is. More arrows—blue ones this time—make a path for us. "This way," I say.

Grandma asks how I know.

"It's just my glasses. They tell me."

"So, you googled it?"

"What? No. Why?" We stare at each other.

Mom—following her glasses' own arrows—charges ahead. "Shall we?"

Once we pass the two-smelling grasshopper place and round the corner to the food court, I hear rock music. Then I see a big sign in the middle of the food court: "MOSH PARTY." Tables and chairs have been cleared away, and in their place, old people are doing exercises? Or dancing? Or fighting? Or play-fighting?

That grasshopper coupon pings up on my lenses again. I close it so I can look up what a mosh party is. Apparently moshing was a kind of dancing in the '90s, where people at a concert would slam into each other on purpose. In the videos I pull up, there's pushing and grabbing and thrashing. It looks like footage from last year's border riots. Why would anyone do that for fun?

But that's not what I'm seeing in front of me right now. All *I'm* seeing is some seniors brushing up against each other with their walkers and canes, and giggling over it. The song they're listening to is snarly though. It's about somebody feeling stupid and contagious, and wanting to be entertained. That's pretty much the only part I can understand. It's the opposite of the songs Mom likes, where somebody's always telling you—very, very clearly—why they're so happy.

A younger woman is sitting at the table where the speakers are set up. Her T-shirt has a smiley face on it, only the smiley face has *X*'s for eyes, and its tongue is lolling out. She sees us staring, smiles, and comes over. She says she's the activity director for The Harbor, the assisted-living facility, but my glasses already told me that. They also told me that her name is April Tran, she's 49, she's a Capricorn, and she buys a lot of Mike and Ike.

April wants to know if we're here for Grunge Day. Because if we're here for Grunge Day, the mosh party just started, and it's open to the public, and she'd love to have us. She looks at Grandma, but Grandma doesn't look at her. No, Grandma looks at the grasshopper place like she's trying to read their menu from 30 feet away—like she doesn't think grasshoppers are disgusting.

Mom nudges Grandma. "Well? Do you want to mosh?" I can't tell if she's joking.

Grandma keeps looking at the grasshopper place. "I was always more of a watermelon-crawl person," she grumbles.

"Oh, country night is next week," April says. "I can get you the information if you want. We're from The Harbor, which is right around the corner there—just past the hairdresser's. It's a convenient location because our residents can pop over for a haircut any day they want. See over there? She's getting the Rachel cut tomorrow, in time for our next 'Must See TV' watch party. If you want, I can get you a couple brochures about—"

"We're going to the pet store now," Grandma says.

"It'll just be a second if you—"

"We're going to the pet store. Now." Grandma starts walking back the way we came.

I whisper, "This way," and steer her in the right direction.

I remember being a little kid and thinking a trip to the pet store was like a field trip to an aquarium. Not that I'd ever been to a real aquarium, but it's how I imagined it would be. Because it didn't matter whether we were at the store to buy fish stuff or not. I mean, we were usually in there to buy live crickets for Mom's green anoles, during that whole reptile phase she had when I was still a little kid. And then, of course, there was: The Ferret.

We never talk about The Ferret.

But I'd always wander over to the fish tanks and tap on the glass and talk to them—*How are you today? Enjoying your bubbling treasure chest? Hey, was that your friend? Because it's bad manners to eat your friend's corpse*—until one day Mom was like, "Don't tap on the glass like that! It scares them!" After that, I'd just slide my finger along the glass to see if any of the fish would follow it while I talked to them, until one day Mom was like, "Don't smudge the glass! Some poor worker has to clean it!" So, after *that*, I'd just stand there with my hands in my pockets and talk to the fish, until one day Mom said, "Don't talk to yourself like that! You look crazy!"

You know, now that I think about it, it's amazing that Mom let me get my goldfish, Callisto, at all.

Even though I'm older now, I still can't help but be like *wow* whenever I see pet-store fish tanks. I don't even *know* how I'd react if I went to a real aquarium. Probably like a dog in one of those "soldier reunited with her pet" videos. All jumpy and tail-waggy.

As soon as we walk into the pet store, my lenses explode with ads for scratching posts, rawhides, kitty litter, and those hamsters. One ad says, "Sale! Female Elephant Ear Betta." When I look at it for long enough, the ad expands to say, "Now $16.99. Was $21.39. Wow!!" and an arrow leads me to the bettas.

We pass some snake habitats: little snakes curled up like spaghetti twirled around your fork; big snakes drooping over fake branches with fake leaves under a fake sun. And Grandma's like *eeek!* and *ack!* and jumping away from them even though there's a sheet of glass between them and her, and even though they're not even moving. And Mom's like, "Oh, please. You're the one who wanted to come to a pet store called United Snakes of America."

"Yeah, but these snakes! They're so close. And so ... snaky. It's outrageous."

We pass a display of driftwood and a display of, I guess, rocks? And then we're there, staring at the glowing wall of fish tanks. And I'm like *wow* all over again.

Freshwater tanks. Saltwater tanks. Freaking *brackish-water* tanks. Snobby-looking angelfish. Meh-looking Oscars. Judgmental-looking fiddler crabs with that one huge claw. Goldfish with bulgy eyes. Goldfish that are black and not gold at all. Goldfish with tails so long and flowy they look like they're wearing evening gowns. Goldfish that look like Callisto and make me sad in a morning-after-Christmas kind of way.

Grandma comes over to the same goldfish tank I'm looking at and asks me how much they are. "No," I tell her. "No goldfish."

"What? Why?"

Is she serious? "Because they need a different water temperature. And you don't have room for them."

She pouts and goes to look at a 100-gallon tank of groupers instead. The groupers are as orange as the icing carrots Mom puts on top of her carrot cakes, and they're covered in bright white polka-dots. They're flashy and glamorous. But they're also a foot long.

"You don't have room for them either, Grandma."

I scan a wall of tanks, and my glasses tell me what's in each one. The labels float over the tanks like speech bubbles in comic books: fire eels, cory catfish, angelfish, zebra danios. Then I see it.

"Grandma! Hey, Grandma! Come over here. Check *this* out."

It's a tank of African dwarf frogs. They're gray with black spots, and they have this facial expression like you just told them a joke. Some of them are paddling around, and some of them are lounging on the turquoise gravel, and a few are floating at the top of the tank.

Grandma looks concerned. "Are they ... ?"

"They're not dead," I say. "They're just relaxing."

She presses her hand against the side of the aquarium. In my head, Mom is saying, *Don't smudge it! Some poor worker has to clean that!* Grandma whispers, "I want them all."

"You can't have them all. You can have, like, one."

"*One?*"

"Yeah, you already have four or five guppies, right?" Or two. Or 20. "You don't want to overstock your tank. It's only a ten-gallon."

"Then let's get a 20-gallon. A *30*-gallon."

Mom steps in: "No. Absolutely not."

"Why not? Give me one good reason."

"Your table's not big enough to hold it. You can't afford it. You can't maintain the tank you already have."

"Give me four good reasons."

Mom runs her fingers through her hair. "How about this?" she says. "How about we buy one frog today—hush, now; just listen for a second—we buy one frog today but we *also* get some new decorations for the tank. Make it look all fresh and new. Renovate."

"Yeah!" I say, probably too cheerfully. "Glazier is telling me there's a cool castle somewhere around here." Actually they've said nothing about a castle, but pet stores always have castles for fish tanks, so fingers crossed. "It'd be like the frog is really a frog-prince, and that's his home."

The wrinkle between Grandma's eyebrows deepens as she considers this. "You mean somebody cursed the prince?"

"Sure."

"And the curse has turned the prince into somebody he doesn't recognize when he looks in the mirror—"

"Uh—"

"But in his heart of hearts, he remembers who he is, even if no one else does."

Across the store, a bird squawks.

"I mean, they also have driftwood," I say.

Mom pats my arm. "Why don't you go find someone who works here so they can get us a frog? Your grandma and I can check out the decorations. But"—she turns to Grandma—"we've got to stop by the hapkido school, remember? So, we should hurry up and get there before they close."

I wander around the sacks of gravel, jars of fish food, and aquarium heaters, looking for someone in a United Snakes of America shirt. I'm passing the gravel vacuums when I think of something: Mom's probably only taking us to this hapkido studio so she has an excuse to hustle Grandma out of the pet store. My shoulders relax, and that's the moment I realize they were tense to begin with. *This is all an act,* I think as I wave down a guy in a T-shirt that says, "Cold Blood, Warm Hearts." *We'll just walk in there and get some info real quick, leave, and never bring it up again. Besides, we probably need to rush home. How long can a frog live in a pet-store baggie of water anyway?*

According to Glazier, an African dwarf frog can live in a baggie of water for *seven to nine hours.*

Which means Callisto might have lived in a baggie of water long enough for us to get to our hotel and set up a temporary aquarium in, like, a storage bin. Which means she could still be alive right now if only I'd remembered to ask Glazier about it instead of leaving her in the aquarium when we evacuated because *obviously* we'd be back the next day. We *always* came back the next day. We'd *never* have to abandon our house and move in with my grandma. That'd be absurd.

But I didn't remember. And now Callisto— the fish I'd had since third grade; the fish I'd talk to about getting 100 on a math quiz or having my braces tightened or lending somebody a comic and not getting it back—is dead.

So, sure, Mom: go ahead and have a long, drawn-out conversation with this old lady in a hapkido uniform while Grandma sits here smiling at her frog and I hold two sacks of gravel, a water-testing kit, tap-water conditioner, a castle, a lava rock, a pod of java moss, and a skull that'll have bubbles coming out of its eye holes.

Grandma leans over and whispers to me, "You should have thought to bring a shopping bag."

I breathe deeply to keep from screaming.

It smells like sixes in here. That's crazy, though, because sixes smell like when you cut the grass, and why would a martial arts studio smell like that? Martial arts studios should smell like sweat and raw hamburger.

The old lady in the hapkido uniform is Master Avery González, age 62, Sagittarius, from Venezuela or maybe Mexico? Glazier can't decide. Her recent purchases include napkin rings and calcium supplements. She's the same woman who was meditating in the ad. In person, she looks like she would own seven Christmas trees, and they'd all have a theme.

Her gray hair is pulled up into a bun, and her gray glasses are tiny octagons, and her gray eyes have Mrs. Claus-looking wrinkles at the corners whenever she smiles.

Her black belt has six white stripes on it, which means she's a sixth-degree black belt, and did you know there were degrees of black-beltedness, and it's not just *black belt, congrats, the end*? Because *I* didn't.

I wonder where the real hapkido teachers are because she must just teach the quote-unquote "hapkido." Or maybe she teaches meditation. Or maybe she teaches tai chi, or whatever that slow martial art for old people is. Or maybe she doesn't teach a martial art at all. Maybe she teaches crocheting. Because that's what she was doing when she stood up to greet us: crocheting. There was a bundle of candy-cane-colored yarn in a basket by her chair, and she was using a crochet hook to loop, loop, loop it into a scarf. Just what every Floridian needs. A scarf.

Mom told her how we're new in town and we saw her ad and we all thought hapkido might be good for me—even though *we all* didn't think anything like that, thank you very much. Then she gave Master Avery her Tourette's Speech: having Tourette's syndrome means I have verbal and motor tics, and I can't always control them, and I'm not trying to be disruptive when I move my arms or repeat a word, and blah blah blah.

Now Master Avery is giving Mom what I can only assume is her Safety Speech: they take safety very seriously here, and they've never had anyone get injured, and the mats they use are the same ones they use in Olympic Judo matches, and on and on.

I zone out and watch the water burbling out of the crane fountain. Then I watch the mist rising out of the oil diffuser that looks like a glowing, green raindrop on the front desk. That must be where the six-ish smell is coming from, the glowing raindrop. Then I peek through the doorway into the next room to see what's in there. Turns out, what's in there—a wall covered in mirrors, a floor covered in oh-so-safe Olympic mats—isn't nearly as interesting as *who's* in there.

A girl in a hapkido uniform is kicking at her reflection. Her kicks are higher than her chin—higher than her head, even. If her foot made contact with your face, you'd be like one of those monsters spitting *ptooey!* in *Black Canary*.

She stops and runs her fingers through her short, black hair to get her bangs out of her face. Then she takes out the stick that's tucked into the front of her brown belt, right behind the knot. It's about as thick as a broom handle and as long as a comic book, actually. She smacks a few imaginary bad guys with it, the way Black Canary smacked that monster with a bowling pin. She slides the stick back into her belt, and I think she's about to do more kicks when her eyes meet mine in the mirror, and time goes elastic. It probably only lasts a second or two—long enough for Master Avery to quote some prices to my mom—but it feels like we're staring at each other for an hour.

She walks toward me. I try to ignore the panic that's sloshing around in my stomach as she passes through the doorway. I look at the glowing raindrop on the desk again.

Grandma nudges me. "She's cute."

"Sssh."

"Get her number."

"*Sssh!*"

Once the girl is right in front of me, I can see that she's wearing earrings—these tiny silver studs. Each one is smaller than one of the white, round sprinkles Mom puts on her nonpareil cookies. If she's wearing any makeup, it's so subtle I can't see it. Now that she isn't in Black Canary mode anymore, she looks kind of plain—like an NPC in one of the video games Grandma watches. You know, one of those blah characters who just wanders around and gets in your way while you try to complete some side quest. And the side quest involves a box that's hidden in this one log—in this one forest—but the box is locked, and to get the key, you have to visit, like, five elves.

"Hi," she says.

"Hi," I say.

"*Hi!*" Grandma says. "What's your name? How old are you? What school do you go to? Do you have a girlfriend?" She frowns. "Or a boyfriend?"

I try to laugh like Grandma's just making a joke, but it sounds so fake—like *HA! HA! HA!*—that I feel myself start to blush. "Oh, Grandma,"

I say, "you're too funny! I *think* her name is Monica Jones, she's 14, and she goes to Plum-Gidley"—at least that's what my glasses says as they measure the angle of her cheekbones or the distance between the tip of her nose and the corner of her mouth or whatever they do— "but there's also, like, a one percent chance she's a young Winona Ryder, so I don't know *what* to believe. HA! HA!"

The girl laughs, but it's a *real* laugh, thank God. "Yeah, everybody always thinks I'm Monica Jones. One of these days, I should meet up with her for a snow cone or something, but apparently she lives in—"

"Sarasota," I say, frowning. "Like, how did I not notice that before?"

"It's OK, don't worry about it. This Monica person always comes up first."

"It's right there, too. In big letters: SARASOTA."

"Seriously, don't worry about it. It happens all the time. You've got to scroll pretty far down to find me. I'm Ruby."

I flip through dossiers until I find her. Ruby Fernández; student at Kimberley E. Nobles

Academy; age 15; born April 24, 2035. Zodiac sign: Taurus. Ancestry, in pie-chart form, although I feel like Glazier gets this wrong most of the time: 31.4 percent Native American, 23.5 percent Iberian, 23.2 percent broadly southern European, 18.5 Scandinavian, 3.1 percent sub-Saharan African, 0.3 percent Ashkenazi. Most recent purchases: a six-pack of microfiber lens wipes, a stapler, period underwear, a glasses case with a deer on it, solar suspenders with constellations on them and *three* charging ports? OK, maybe I should buy those suspenders myself. I wonder if you can get them in any other patterns besides the constellation one.

I flag the suspenders to check them out later and realize I haven't been listening to a word Ruby is saying.

"It's weird," she's saying now. "I guess I just have one of those faces. But maybe when anybody meets Monica Jones, they think she's me and start asking her what it's like to go to Nobles. Who knows? Anyway, what's *your* name?"

"I'm Louisa. But can't you just ... ?" I point to my own glasses.

"Oh, yeah, it's a rule here. We have to turn all that off during class. We can only have the emergency alerts on, like 'Oh, no! There's a fire!' or 'Look out! Tornado! *Blargh!*' And absolutely no recording."

"Oh!"

"Yeah."

"I forget they're even recording," I say. "They're just, like, there."

"Yeah. Same here. The other option is, you can just take your glasses off, which is simpler. That's what I'd do if I could, but mine are prescription, so you know, I'm basically stuck with them."

"Oh."

"Because I can't wear contacts. Because they make my eyes hurt."

"Oh."

We both stare at the frog in Grandma's lap. Now there's a thick, black pause spreading over our conversation like an oil spill.

I swallow hard. "I wear con—"

"You're starting up a—Oh, sorry, I interrupted you."

"No, no," I say. "It's—"

"You go. No, you talk."

"No, it's stupid, what I was going to say, really. *You* talk."

But something about the way I say "*You* talk" isn't quite right. What's wrong is the pitch: it needs to swoop higher at the end, almost like a question. Instead, it dipped low.

I know it's stupid. I know it doesn't matter. But it's giving me anxiety. That's my other about-to-have-a-tic feeling: this anxiety over sounds. It feels like when you're peeling open a can of biscuit dough and you're getting closer and closer to the moment it explodes.

So, I clear my throat and say it again: "*You* talk?" Maybe she'll just think I'm being exceedingly polite.

We stare at the frog again.

For once, Grandma embarrasses me and I'm actually grateful for it: she asks me if my glasses can tell me whether Ruby has a boyfriend or a girlfriend, or not.

Ruby smiles. And, you know what? I take back everything I said about her looking like an NPC. I was wrong. She looks like a proper main character. I mean, she's unique, you know? She stands out, and I'm not even sure why.

She tells Grandma, "I'm not seeing anyone, no." Then she looks at me and says, "Are you starting here?"

"Yes. No. I mean, maybe I am."

"Of course she's starting here," Grandma says. "Now, tell me, Riley—"

"*Ruby*," I mutter.

"—when does she get to break boards with her head?"

Ruby laughs. "We don't break boards with our heads here. Or with our hands. Or with, like, anything. But that *does* sound exciting."

"Well, when does she get to hit people with sticks?" She points to the stick tucked into Ruby's belt.

"Oh, we don't learn short-stick techniques until brown belt. I just earned *my* brown belt a few weeks ago. It took me about two years to get there from white belt."

I nod toward Mom, who's talking to Master Avery about self-esteem. "In two years," I tell Ruby in a low voice, "I'm pretty sure I'll still be sitting here, holding all this stuff."

"Yeah, what *is* all this? You starting up a fish tank, or what?"

"We're renovating the fish tank my grandma already has. I think the water parameters are—Never mind."

"No! What is it?"

"Never mind. It's boring."

She chants, "Say it. *Say it. Say it! SAY IT!*"

"OK, OK, well, imagine you have this fish tank, right? And you want to make sure all your fish and plants don't die. You have to make sure your water parameters are all within a normal range. So, for one thing, you have to be sure the water isn't too alkaline, which means—"

"A pH that's higher than seven."

"Right."

"Because seven is neutral."

"Right!"

"You know, it sounds a lot like—"

"All right, y'all, I think we're ready to go," Mom says. She takes the skull, the lava rock, and the water conditioner from me and balances them on top of the white bundle she's now carrying. It takes me a second to realize the bundle is a uniform.

Ruby holds up her index finger like *wait*. "Be right back." She jogs into the room with all the mats.

Mom looks at me, confused, but I ignore it: "Did you sign me up? Am I actually doing this?"

"You look a lot happier about it than you did a minute ago, *that's* for sure."

"OK, but am I doing it or not?"

"You start next Tuesday, after school. The first three lessons will be private. Just you and Master Avery. She'll teach you a few basic techniques, some easy kicks—things like that. Then you'll be in the regular class with everybody else."

"*Everybody* else? Including the brown belts? I mean what I mean is, it won't just be me and the other beginners, will it? Or, *will* it?"

"Oh, for heaven's sake, Louisa, I don't know. She made it sound like it'd be everybody, OK? But if you want to know so bad, why don't you go ask her?" She gestures to Master Avery, who's gone back to crocheting.

"Forget about it."

"But you can just ask—"

"I said forget about it."

Ruby returns with an unzipped backpack. It has a NASA logo on it, and there's a rainbow of tiny, crocheted keychains hanging from the zipper pull. I think they're awareness ribbons for bringing home the troops or getting screened for mental health disorders or *oh! Oh!* I know what they are now! They're little hapkido belts. They look just like the ones displayed on the wall behind the front desk: white, yellow, orange, green, blue, and brown. And the belt that comes after all *that* is black.

"Here," Ruby says. She holds the backpack out to me. "You need this more than I do today."

I say, "No, no. It's fine. I've got it, really," at the same time that Mom says, "How sweet of you to offer!" and Grandma says, "If I put the frog in there, do you think the baggie will pop?"

"Take it," Ruby says. "Just take it. When you have your next lesson, you can bring it back. You can leave it for me by the shoe rack if I'm not around."

What shoe rack? "OK."

She helps me pack everything into the bag except for the frog, which Grandma keeps, and the castle, which Mom holds because it's fragile. "I forgot to ask," she says, holding the backpack up so I can slip it on. "What's your name anyway?"

"Louisa." I brace myself for her to joke about the hurricane, but she doesn't. It's exactly the reaction somebody would have had before the storm came and ruined my life: no reaction at all.

"Well, Louisa," she says, tightening the shoulder straps, "how does that feel?"

"Good," I say. "Really good."

# CHAPTER 5

It's one thing to sleep in Grandma's guestroom when I'm full of turkey and cornbread dressing and sweet potato casserole, and I can smell Mom's chocolate-pecan pie warming in the oven, and I can hear Mom and Grandma in the living room, watching *A Christmas Story* for the thousandth time and laughing over a game of Spoons.

But it's a whole other thing to sleep in Grandma's guestroom when it's technically my bedroom, and I'm full of ranch grasshoppers—which were a terrible idea—and my arm tics are acting up, and I can hear the play-through Grandma's watching. Fourth of July music is seeping through the wall. Somebody yells, "Make ready! Present! Fire!" and muskets blast.

Resisting the urge to flail my arms is like having a fire-ant bite and not being able to scratch it. You just have to let the itch happen. But I know that little by little, day by day, all the resisting I do is turning me into a stronger person. It's giving me more discipline, and it's building my character, and ha ha, just kidding, it's terrible and I hate it, and there is absolutely nothing good about it. At all. I don't care *what* my mom or my therapist says.

I fold my arms across my stomach and tense up all my arm muscles at the same time. Silently, I start counting backward: *100 ... 99 ...* My therapist is the one who suggested I do this to keep my arm tics under control. He calls it a "competing response." But by the time I get to 45, it's still not working because who is he fooling? It only works part of the time.

I go ahead and tic out—get it out of my system—and turn on the lamp by the bed. I fumble with my contact lens case, pop my contacts in, and put my glasses on. It's five past 11.

All the clutter surrounding me leaps out of the half-dark: a Reba McEntire T-shirt hanging from a treadmill; a 2-D printer that Ruby's backpack is slumped against; a stack of jigsaw puzzles that are probably missing pieces; an autographed poster of Lorrie Morgan, whoever that is; a third-place trophy for barrel racing sharing desk space with my figurines.

In the kitchen, somebody—it's got to be Grandma—is banging pots and pans around. In the living room, a cannon booms.

I text Ezra. "Hey. Are you up?" Then, before he can even write back: "Mom signed me up for a martial art." No response. "Longest day EVER." Still no response.

Just when I've decided he must really be asleep, a page from the comic he's working on—in itty-bitty, dollhouse size—blips into the corner of my right lens. I expand it. The Shaman, wearing his antlered hat, is walking through a forest where the trees have eyes.

"I'm up," he texts. "Working on this piece of trash."

"It's not trash!"

"It's confusing. My eye doesn't know where to go. Ergo, trash."

"Oh, if you say ERGO, it must be true."

"I need to simplify. Be minimalist. Like those Japanese prints. With the flowers. That's what Lydia does. It's cool."

My stomach feels like I'm on an elevator that's plunging from the penthouse to the ground floor. I text, "Who's Lydia?"

For a sea of time that's probably no more than a raindrop of actual time, Ezra doesn't answer. Then he's like, "Just a girl in my club."

"You have a CLUB?"

"An illustration club."

Now it's my turn to not answer.

He texts, "It's just a thing some of us in art class decided to do."

"OK."

"Why do you have to be like that?"

Grandma drops a pan. It clangs like a cymbal.

"Hey," I text, "I had the craziest dream last night." I want to talk about something else. Anything else.

"Are we OK?"

"We were at the beach. It was the picnic again. Only with all these clouds. And lightning."

My glasses buzz in my ear. Ezra is calling. I take it, but I don't even say hello. I just keep describing my dream to him: "I was like, 'We should go home,' but you were like, 'Nah, this is fine,' even though the wind was whipping my hair around my face. And the ocean swelled until there was this wall of water headed for us, but you acted like you didn't see it—like nothing bad was happening—but when *I* looked at the wave, I could kind of see through it. Not the way you can see through a window but more like how you can see through ... Jell-O? And inside the wave, there was all this stuff I didn't take with me before the storm came, and I could see it all perfectly: that rattly peacock I had since I was a baby, my—"

"Stop it," Ezra whisper-yells. "I mean, I love you. But stop it. I'm going to meet people. Some of those people are going to become my friends. That's life. I'm sorry, but that's just life. And you're going to meet people, too—"

"I know you're going to have friends. Duh. I'm not saying you can't."

"Some of those people are going to be *your* friends." Ruby pops into my head: *A pH that's higher than seven. Because seven is neutral.* "But that doesn't mean they're boyfriends or girlfriends. And no matter what friends I—"

"Ezra!" his mama says. "What did I tell you?"

"Mama, I know, but just—"

"Glasses off. To bed."

"Just let—"

"*To. Bed.*"

Ezra sighs. He tells me we'll talk tomorrow.

His mama calls out, "You go to sleep, too, Louisa."

But I don't. As soon as Ezra and I say good night, I try to find out who Lydia is.

After a few minutes of help from Glazier, I'm pretty sure she fosters homeless kittens. At least, if she's the Lydia I *think* she is, she does. If she's the other Lydia, she cooks pork chops in a real-life chuck wagon. Which seems unlikely.

There's a picture of her with a black-and-white kitten perched on the back of the couch, halfway behind her curly, blonde hair. She's like, "Meet Cecil," cat-with-bowtie emoji. "He's my newest foster. Don't let his formal appearance fool you: he may be a tuxedo cat, but he loves to romp and play."

I find a video of her balling up a piece of foil and flicking it across the kitchen so an orange kitten can skitter after it. I play the video back, pause it, and zoom in on her dangly earrings that look like silver peapods. Then I look at the pocket on her sleeve and wonder what's inside. Could be anything, really. Lip balm? Gum? A switchblade? Cash stolen from a cancer treatment collection jar? Who can say? I mean, her shopping history could have all *kinds* of psycho things on it. Violent things. Illegal things. Things like ... OK, she bought vegan cat treats. And made a donation to the Humane Society. And *oh!* I think she bought marijuana! And she's only 14, so she's totally not old enough for—Oh, hold on. Never mind. That's catnip.

Well, maybe her art is bad, at least.

Nope. It's good.

Most of it looks like charcoal drawings of fruit bowls and flowers in vases. Some of it is paintings—maybe India-ink paintings?—of a single branch of a cherry tree or, like, one bird. And there will be a ton of blank space surrounding it, right? It's what Ezra said it was: minimalist. It's calming. It's thoughtful. It's an oasis.

I hate it.

I clear my lenses and walk, squinting, into the kitchen, where Grandma's sitting on the floor and taking pots and pans out of a cabinet.

When I ask what she's doing, she says, "Making horn-of-plenty muffins. Or, *trying* to. I can't find my muffin tin." She pulls out a sheet pan; a skillet falls out. She pulls out a loaf pan; a saucepan falls out. "And this!" she says, holding up a booklet. "Why is this in here? This is the user manual for an electric toothbrush." She flings it across the room.

"Do you normally cook in the middle of the night?"

"I'm retired. I do what I want."

I squat next to her and stretch my nightgown over my legs so only my toes are peeking out. "Hey, so, have you ever hated somebody even though there's nothing wrong with them?"

"Of course. I'm old. Hate is what's keeping me alive."

"Grandma!"

"What do you mean, '*Grandma!*'? It's true. I hate my doctor because she's always saying my mind's not right, but you know the only reason she says that? The AI. Because all these doctors do anymore—especially these *Gen Alpha* doctors—all they do is ask the AI. Trust the AI. Hail the AI. They're so 'AI this' and 'AI that' that they don't actually learn anything in med school. They just learn how to ask the AI." She shakes her head. "A scam. It's *all* a scam. All of it. These doctors, I mean: what do they know? Really! What do they *know*? I'll tell you what they know: nothing. Me, on the other hand? I know some things. I've been around for a good, long while. I'm old enough to remember when computers took floppy disks. I'm old enough to remember when restaurants had ashtrays."

"What's an—?"

"I'm old enough to remember when people asked you for the time. I'm old enough to remember Crystal Pepsi. I'm old enough to remember when there were two Germanys. Anyway ... what were we talking about?"

"Hate."

"Right. Hate. Now, why are you asking about that? You're too young to have any hate."

"I guess what I really mean is, have you ever disliked someone even though they're a good person and they probably wouldn't even dislike *you* if they had the chance? Like, have you ever wanted to get revenge on them even though they haven't done anything that needs to be avenged?"

"Sure. Like, maybe you want to tell them off while everybody watches."

"Right! Or maybe you want to—I don't know—leave comments on their posts that could seem nice or sarcastic, depending on how they read them."

"Or leave a comment that says nobody loves them, nobody ever has loved them, and nobody ever will love them, until the day they die."

"Wait, what? No. That's kind of messed up."

"Or—*or*—you could set up your own fake account, leave nice comments on their posts, gain their trust over a year or so, plan a trip with them to Everglades National Park, rent a canoe when you get there, take them way out into Florida Bay, and—"

"You know what? No. Let's just not."

"*You* brought it up, Miss Priss. Oh, look! A puzzle piece. Why don't you help your grandma out and put this in the box when you go back to your room later?"

I have no idea what puzzle it belongs to. It's part of a sky, but pretty much all of the puzzles in my room involve a sky. "Sure."

"I know what you need. What *you* need is a hate shower."

"Is this something people did when you were my age?"

"It's something *I* did when I was your age. When I'd get really mad at somebody—or about something—I'd lock myself in the bathroom, take a quick shower, get out, and put on my robe. That robe was so fluffy. It felt like wearing a stuffed animal. Anyway. I'd put on my fluffy robe, and I'd leave the shower running, and I'd sit on the floor—we had this lavender rug; I'd sit on that—and watch the whole bathroom turn into a steam room—"

"Ew! Wasn't the rug wet? And gross? I feel like bathroom rugs are always wet and gross. Like, have you ever gotten down and smelled one?"

"Of course not. Who would smell a rug?"

"Not me." Grandma's bathroom rug smells like when you carve a jack-o-lantern. "I just mean, was the rug actually comfortable to sit on?"

"I don't know why you're fixated on the rug."

"I'm not fixated on the rug."

"The rug was fine, all right? The rug was a rug. But I'd sit there, and I'd imagine all the rage inside of me was a piece of red-hot iron— the gooey kind you can put on an anvil and hit with a hammer. And I'd imagine the steam surrounding me was the water bath a blacksmith puts a piece of iron in once they're done shaping it and they want to harden it. At least I *think* that's how it works. Anyway, this was before the water rationing started—way,

*way* before all that—so I swear I'd sit in there for an hour sometimes, just hardening. And when I was done, I'd feel ready to take care of whatever needed taken care of. Or *whoever* needed taken care of.

"So, if I was mad because your great-grandma got onto me for having a messy room—you know, for instance—I'd clean my room, all right. I'd clean it *too* well. Malicious compliance. I'd drag out every cleaning product in the house and slam things around and run the vacuum while she was trying to watch *Frasier*. And the whole time, I wouldn't even feel mad anymore. I'd feel really, really calm. But also really, really ready to fight. I don't know how to put it. I just don't know."

"But wouldn't it get boring in there, just sitting on a rug for an hour? Would you even take your glasses—or your phone or whatever—in there with you?"

"Well, sometimes I'd watch the fish tank."

"You had a fish tank in the bathroom?"

"Yeah, there was this little table in there where your great-grandma would keep her makeup and lotion and stuff in these little drawers, and on top of it was a fish tank. Sixty-gallon, maybe?" There is no way a 60-gallon tank could fit on top of a makeup table, but fine, moving on. "Because, you know, I didn't always live in a mobile home. When I was growing up, we lived in a white house with a fence in front, and all these sunflowers." I picture a pop-up book being opened, with a flat, paper house and a flat, paper fence painted with sunflowers rising up off the page. I also picture a weathervane that actually turns. I don't know why. "We kept this 60- or 70-gallon fish tank in the bathroom. There was Spongebob's pineapple house in it—you know who Spongebob is, right?—and this scuba diver who went up and down. And we had these ... well, I *want* to say they were rainbow fish, but now I'm not sure."

I ask my glasses to show me a rainbow fish. The fish that appears on my lenses has shimmery, greenish-blue scales, like a mermaid. Or, oh! No! You know what it's like? It's like Mera's bodice! And its tail and dorsal fin are as red as Mera's hair. It's Mera's spirit animal.

I ask Grandma, "Did they look like this?" I take my glasses off and hold them out to her. She stares at them like I'm handing her a snapping turtle. "Go ahead. Try them on." She reaches out but stops with her hand halfway between us. "Go *ahead*. You won't break them, if that's what you're worried about."

She takes off her own glasses—the Ben Franklin kind that only make things look clearer—and folds them in her lap. Then she puts on mine. Her mouth falls open. "Holy Hannah."

"Is that what your fish looked like?"

"Holy Hannah."

"Hey. You want to see something really cool? *OK, Glazier: What does a dog see?*"

Grandma gasps. "Everything's ... everything's gray!"

"*OK, Glazier: What does a bee see?*"

She waves her hand in front of her face. "It's all pixels. And they're glowing."

"Uh-huh."

"They're really *glowing*. Ack! What's happening?"

"If you move your fingers in front of the lenses like that, it advances to the next animal. What do you see?"

"I don't know how to explain it. It's like I can see everything, all at the same time. Front, left, right. All of it. Even some of the fridge behind me."

"Ah. Must be the horse."

Slowly she stands up. She creeps around the kitchen with one hand sliding along the counter, the sink, the dishwasher. "You mean this is what Angel saw?"

"Who's Angel?"

"My horse."

"You had a *horse*?"

"Of course I had a horse." She giggles. "That rhymes."

"I don't think you can say 'of course' about something like that."

"We competed, Angel and me."

"In what?"

"Rodeo." She turns around and walks back the way she came, gripping the counter some more. "Barrel racing was my best event. Placed in it a few times, believe it or not."

"You mean you actually *won* that barrel-racing trophy in my room? I thought you found it at an antique store or something."

"No way. That trophy is all mine. I would have been—let's see—21 when I won it. Or maybe twen—Oh!" She kicks a saucepot over. The lid clatters to the ground.

The door to the den creaks open, and Mom lurches out, pulling the earplugs out of her ears. "What's going on out here?"

"Baking?" I say.

"Bella! *Bella!* I can see you from here even though I'm facing the sink! At least, I *think* I'm facing the sink." Grandma waves in Mom's general direction. "Hi, Bella!"

I try to explain: "I couldn't sleep, so I came out here, and Grandma was looking for her muffin tin—"

"Why were you making muffins in the middle of the night?" Mom asks her.

I mutter, "That's what *I* said."

Grandma takes my glasses off. She sets them on the counter. "Well, really, Isabella, it's nobody else's business how I spend my—"

"Why is the stove on?"

"The stove isn't on. It's the oven that's on. I'm preheating it."

Mom points to the stove knob that's turned up to HIGH, the way an Arabic teacher would point to a letter on the board and have everyone say, "*Alif.*" She flicks the knob to OFF. Then she holds her hand a few inches over the left front burner and shakes her head. "This burner was *on*. I'm telling you."

"Like I said, it's nobody's business when I bake. Before y'all came here—and don't get me wrong, I love you, and I'm happy you're here—but before y'all came here, I baked whatever I wanted to, whenever I wanted to, and nobody said a thing about it, and I was getting along just fine. Wasn't I getting along just fine? Yeah. You *know* I was getting along just fine."

"Wrecking your car twice in one month isn't exactly 'getting along just fine,' Mom."

I straitjacket myself in my arms. *99 ... 98 ...*

Grandma points to the den that's now Mom's bedroom. Her neck—around the hollow of her throat—is turning red. "Used to be, I was going to turn that room into a home gym, where I was going to do my physical therapy—my PT. I was going to get a rowing machine and everything. Prove those doctors wrong. Show them there's nothing wrong with me."

Mom puts her hands on her hips. "Oh, *were* you now?"

"What? You don't believe me?"

"Oh, I believe you'd buy a rowing machine. I just don't believe you'd use it."

I think of Mom's crème brûlée torch, but I don't say anything.

Grandma slams her hand against the counter. The salt-and-pepper shakers—shaped like a bear hugging a honey pot—jump. And honestly? So do I. "This is bullcrap."

Every muscle and tendon and ligament in my arms wants me to throw my arms in the air. It's like they're all whispering to me at the same time, "Do it!" *84 ... 83 ...*

"You don't even use the elastic bands—"

"Bullcrap." *Slam.*

*80 ... 79 ...*

"I invite y'all into my home—I turn my life upside down—and this is what I have to put up with? My own daughter, treating me like a kid? Acting like I can't live independently? Make my own choices? Do things for myself? Bullcrap." *Slam.* "Louisa, here's your glasses, baby." She holds them out to me. "I'm going to take a shower. A nice, long shower." A hate shower. "You think I'm not independent? I'm independent."

She stomps forward, but then she freezes. She picks up her foot. She's stepped on her glasses—her might-as-well-be-from-the-1800s glasses—and now one of the arms is bent at a weird angle. She tries to bend it back into place, but when she puts the glasses on again, they're so crooked that I have to hold my breath to keep from laughing. She flounces out of the room, but a trail of blood drops follows her all the way to her master bedroom, where her bathroom is. She cut her foot. How can she not feel it?

Mom grabs the rooster-print dishtowel that's slung over the oven-door handle. She starts to wipe up the blood. "The perfect end to a perfect day."

"And it's only Day One."

"What?"

"We've only been here one day."

"*What?* No. That can't be right." She stops wiping and looks up at me, wide-eyed. "God, I'm so tired. Can that be right?"

"No, actually," I say. "I'm wrong." She turns her attention back to the floor. *Scrub, scrub, scrub.* "It's only been nine hours."

# CHAPTER 6

If silence had a color, it would be as white as my hapkido uniform.

It's so white that you can kind of see my flowery underwear through the drawstring pants. Mom says the top half of the uniform covers it, but *I* say all I have to do is move the wrong way and *surprise!* And she says, "Then don't move that way."

"Oh, thanks. *That's* helpful."

"Well, if it bothers you so much, you should have changed your underwear before we left the house. What do you want me to do about it now? We're already in the—Doing great, Master Avery! How are *you*?"

Master Avery bows as she shakes Mom's hand. Then she bows as she shakes *my* hand. And she tells us that bowing is a sign of respect, and it doesn't have anything to do with religion or kings and queens. It's just the etiquette here in the *dojang*.

But we don't just bow "hello" to each other, Master Avery explains. She says we also bow "goodbye" to each other. And we bow when we enter the *dojang*, like Ruby just did—hi, Ruby! you're here early—and we bow when we leave. We bow when we walk into the mat room, and we bow when we walk out of it. We bow before we step onto the mat. We bow before we step *off* of the mat. We bow before we practice with someone—as a promise not to hurt them—and we bow when we're done practicing with them. She asks Ruby if she's forgetting anything.

Ruby looks up from her chair, where she's unbuckling her sandal. "We bow when we hand someone a knife."

*A knife?*

"Ah!" Master Avery says. "Good! We bow when we hand something to someone, or when someone hands something to us. You know, Ruby, I'm glad you're here. You can show Louisa and her mom—this is her mom, Ms. Weber—where the shoe rack is. Then we can all meet up in the little mat room so you can show them what it looks like to fall."

Hold on.

"Because we get thrown in here, Louisa."

Hang on just a minute.

"And it's important that we fall correctly so we don't get injured."

Excuse me: can we go back to the part where you said I'd get *thrown?*

"And the more we practice falling, the better we do it, and the less scary it is."

"It's true," Ruby says, leading Mom and me into the big mat room. "The first time I fell in here, I thought I'd have a heart attack, but now it's as natural as riding a bike."

I almost blurt out that I never learned how to ride a bike without training wheels, but I stop myself just in time. Instead, I say, "Hey, I brought your backpack." As we cross the big mat room, I slide it off my shoulder and hand it to her. She bows as she takes it from me, but I don't remember to. Great. I couldn't even get *that* right.

"Did you forget something in here?" Ruby gently shakes the backpack. Something *shooshes* around inside.

"Oh," I say. "That." I look down at the chipped, black polish on my toenails and wish I'd thought to touch it up.

Mom clasps her hands in front of her chest. "You were an angel to us the other day. An absolute angel. And I don't believe in returning a pie pan empty or gifting anybody a purse without a little something tucked inside. So, I made you a batch of SunButter chocolate chip cookies."

"Aw, y'all didn't need to do all *that*." She looks at both of us, even though I didn't have anything to do with the cookies.

"You can keep the tin," Mom says.

"Y'all are too sweet!"

I mumble, "Mom likes to bake." She's always doing this: making grand gestures and foisting baked goods on people. It's obnoxious. Like, just say *thank you* for once in your life.

Ruby says we'll have to send her the recipe later. She says her little sister loves to bake, but she usually just uses cake mixes and stuff, so it'll be fun for her to make something from scratch. Of course, she's only six, so she's too young to bake anything on her own—like, *way* too young—but their mom and dad help her, and sometimes Ruby does, too, but only after she bugs her about it. Because the thing is, Ruby isn't into baking—not that there's anything *wrong* with baking—so she reminds herself that baking is essentially a science experiment, and sorry, she's rambling, just yap yap yap, she's always rambling like that, and should she confirm her number for me? You know: to send her the recipe?

Ruby smiles, which is a relief because *"Should you confirm your number for me?"* is like something an alien would say if it were trying to pass as a human. I'm shocked Ruby actually exchanges numbers with me—*"Should you confirm your number for me?"* seriously?—before Mom and I go to the "little mat room."

The little mat room looks a lot like the big one only it's, you know, *little*. There's a smaller cluster of mats in the middle of the floor—not much bigger than a king-size bed—and a smaller wall of mirrors that reminds me of a dressing room.

Mom and I sit at the glass-topped table in the corner, and oh, wonderful: now the glass is like some shrapnel grenade in the play-throughs Grandma watches. Because all I can think about is, it sure would be bad if I had an arm tic right about now. It sure would be bad if I smacked the table with my charm bracelet. Sure would be bad if the big conch-shell charm shattered the glass and I cut myself and everybody screamed and there was blood everywhere and good Lord, why do I even think these things?

Master Avery and Ruby bow onto the mat. Master Avery asks her, "How many times do you think you've been thrown in this *dojang*?"

"Let's see. I've been going here three times a week, for a little over two years. At least, I *think* it's been more than two years. So how many classes is that? A little over 300? And let's say I get thrown an average of five—"

Master Avery lays a hand on her arm. "Would it be fair to say you've been thrown hundreds of times?"

"Oh, sure! Definitely, ma'am."

"So if I threw you right now, would you be scared?"

"No, ma'am, not at—"

But before she can finish, Master Avery has wrapped one arm around her waist and slammed her on the mat. Ruby lands with a thud—it's the sound a full laundry basket makes when you drop it on the floor—and lies there laughing for a second before she gets up like nothing even happened. The only difference is her uniform has shifted just enough that I can see part of a tattoo beneath her collarbone. It's a wavy, black-and-orange something-or-other. But that can't be, can it? How does Miss Sprinkle Earrings have a tattoo?

Master Avery turns to me. "That's what you and *I* are going to work on today. Falls."

"I'm going to fall like that? I mean, like that?"

"Not like *that*. You'll be learning a simple back fall, starting from the ground. But that's what you'll work your way up to. So, Ruby, why don't you go warm up before your class starts? Louisa and I are going to work on our back falls together. Oh, and Ruby? One more thing." Master Avery grabs her own earlobes and wiggles them.

Ruby grabs hers, too, feels the earrings, and smiles. "Got it!" She bounds out of the room.

I must look confused.

"Ruby got her ears pierced about two weeks ago, but we don't want her earrings to get caught on something. Students who can't take their piercings out just cover them with tape or band-aids. Now then ..."

Master Avery sits on the mat, looks at me, and pats the space next to her like *have a seat.*

Sitting on the mat is nothing like sitting on a bed, which is what I had imagined. It's more like sitting on a huge, flexed muscle. Master Avery tells me to put my legs straight out, like hers. She tells me to cross my arms, tuck my chin close against my chest, fall backward, and slap the mat really hard. "Like this." Her slap is so loud that it hangs in the air, like when you drop a glass, and it shatters, and the world stops turning for a second. "You try it. Really, go ahead. Try it."

*Big slap*, I think.

Little slap is what I do.

But Mom applauds, even though I know I didn't do it right. *"OK, Glazier,"* she says. *"Take a picture.* I'm sending *this* one to your grandma. It might distract her from how sick she feels today."* Mom hardly ever fan-girls over me like this. The last time it happened, I had correctly IDed almond extract in the leftover birthday cake Mom brought home from work, when the only letters left on it were HA BIRT ISA.

"Hey!" Master Avery says. "Good job keeping your chin tucked."

"Really?"

"Really. That's the most important thing—to protect your head—and you did it perfectly. All you have to do now is a *big* slap. Say it after me: *big* slap."

*"Big* slap."

"The louder the slap, the safer you are. Got it?"

"Got it."

"Try again?"

I look at myself in the mirror. With my arms crossed across my chest, I almost look like I'm waiting out a tic. This time when I fall, I slap so hard my fingers sting.

Master Avery nods. "Let's do it 10 more times, OK? On my count. One."

My imagination smells burning hair: the smell of hair appointments and being someone's junior bridesmaid, the smell of hot rollers, straightening wands, and curling irons plugged into outlets next to bathroom sinks, warming scalps, burning ears, tugging individual hairs so hard it makes your eyes water. *Slap.*

"Two."

That's the smell of carnival food and buckets of chicken and hash browns in greasy, little paper sleeves. *Slap.*

"Three."

The smell of ice cream sandwich wrappers. *Slap.*

"Four."

The smell of Kleenex and illness and *The Price Is Right* on a Wednesday morning and an idiot saying that a bag of tortilla chips costs more than the cold medicine you're on right now.

"Five."

The smell of the Japanese restaurant Mom and I went to every Saturday: soy sauce and—I don't know—rice, I guess? And when we were done eating, we'd stand by the goldfish pond they had out front and watch the orange-and-white fish swirling in the murk while we snapped our fortune cookies open—because, yeah, they gave us fortune cookies for some reason, even though that's a Chinese thing, not a Japanese thing—and read our fortunes to each other. Sometimes, before we actually opened the cookies, we'd announce some funny phrase we had to add to the end of it. Like "after the procedure" or "on the toilet." So: "Kindness is one of your best attributes after the procedure" and "This too shall pass on the toilet."

It was just a little thing we did, back when we were normal. I think that might be why I got Callisto. I loved those goldfish in that pond. No matter what was happening in my life—whether I threw my pen across the classroom during an arm tic, or the COVID shot was a bad match that year and I got sick anyway—I always knew the fish were still doing their little fishy things in their little fishy pond. And that was nice to think about.

And as I throw myself back on the mat, tucking my chin and watching my feet fly into the air, I realize I know what Ruby's tattoo is. *Slap!*

It's a goldfish.

# CHAPTER 7

All of the kicks have numbers, and when one of those numbers is linked to one of my imaginary smells, it makes it easier for me to memorize it. So, take kick number eight. It's the high heel front kick, and it goes to the bad guy's chin. I can remember that because, whenever I practice kick eight, I think of how my mom's snickerdoodles smell. Because snickerdoodles and eights both smell like cinnamon.

Kick two—the diagonal snapping toe kick— goes for the armpit. It smells like fried food: funnel cakes and tempura grasshoppers.

And kick one is the shin kick, the smells-like-burning-hair kick. To do it, your opponent has to be standing close to you. That means that kick one can be a little bit sneaky. One minute, you're talking. The next minute, *bam*. It's a hard candy that looks like green apple but tastes like wasabi. It's a spider under your pillow. It's a gift bag full of wasps.

# CHAPTER **8**

Ezra says hapkido wouldn't work in a real fight. "It only works if the bad guy cooperates. Not if he resists you."

I slouch down in my desk, pretend to read my bio textbook, and text him back: "Have YOU done any hapkido?" I mean, sure, I've only done three private lessons, but that's three more lessons than *he's* done.

He doesn't answer.

"OK, then," I say. Laughing-dolphin emoji.

"I've been watching a lot of MMA. To help me illustrate fight scenes in the Shaman. And the pros never do hapkido. They do Muay Thai or BJJ. Brazilian jiu-jitsu."

"I know what BJJ is."

At the front of the classroom, Ms. Perez clears her throat dramatically. "*Louisa,*" she says. "Are you with us?"

"Yes. Yes, ma'am."

"I can see you texting with your eyes. I'm not blind."

She hands out the worksheets. They have fill-in-the-blank questions about fishing, like "People have fished for red *blank* in the Gulf of Mexico since the 1840s" and "The largest species of fish is the *blank* shark."

You'd *think* learning about fish would be interesting—for me, at least—but Ms. Perez has managed to make it even more boring than the time she went on and on about plant cells and chloroplasts.

She tells the board to play *Hooked*, and a video called *Hooked: A History of Fishery Management in the Gulf of Mexico* starts. Its copyright date is 2021. Everyone looks like they just stepped out of my mom's seventh-grade yearbook: so many pairs of high-waisted jeans and round glasses frames; so many eyebrows as thick as caterpillars.

We're supposed to fill out the worksheet based on what we learn from this video, but when Ms. Perez turns the lights off—so we can see the screen better—I can hardly read the paper anymore. I put my glasses into reading mode so the letters on the worksheet look bigger and crisper. I also make the paper look black and the words look white, because that helps, too.

What's the largest species of fish? The whale shark.

What have people fished for in the Gulf since the 1840s? Red snapper.

What Native American tribe fished in the Gulf? The Apalachees. But that question is stupid because, for one thing, you know other tribes were catching fish too and, for another thing, the Apalachees are still around, so why does this movie make it sound like they disappeared before the telephone was invented?

Which fish learned that whenever I turned on the aquarium light, it was time for breakfast? Callisto.

Who has a goldfish tattoo on her chest? Ruby.

How is Grandma's aquarium doing at this very moment? When I syphoned out most of the gross water and put clean water in, was it too big of a change? Did I shock the fish? Or the frog? I have no idea.

Wondering if the fish are doing OK gives me low-grade, 99.5-degree anxiety. I count; I straitjacket myself. You know, the usual. But it doesn't matter. My arms flail. They flail again. Someone behind me laughs and tries to cover the laugh with a cough. Someone else whispers, "Look at her arms. Just wait. Watch." I flail again. I can't help it. The girl laughs and doesn't even bother to pretend she's coughing. I feel fizzy with anxiety—like a can of panic that's been shaken up but hasn't been opened yet.

Ms. Perez asks if there's a problem, ladies. They say no and try to act normal, but I can hear them trying not to laugh—or, really, I can feel them trying not to laugh. I hug myself so tight that when I breathe in, my ribs can't expand all the way. I rock back and forth in my seat. That makes it creak.

The quote-unquote "ladies" giggle again. Ms. Perez bangs on her desk with her indestructible "Love Can Build a Bridge" mug and snaps, "That's enough!"

Have you ever stormed out of a classroom before? Yeah, me either. At least, not until now. I'm here to tell you that storming out is the easy part. Everything that comes after that is awkward. You're standing in the hallway, not knowing where to go or what to do with yourself or how long you should wait before you go back in because you *have* to go back in at some point, right?

I just squint at the wall of yellow lockers for a while, as my eyes adjust to the light after being in the movie-theater dark for so long. Once I can see like normal again, I look left; I look right. Nobody's around. No tennis shoes squeaking on the floor, no locker doors banging shut. And—this is the part that surprises me—nobody's following me out of the room to see if I'm OK or send me to the principal's office or call me a Loosa or anything. So I take the opportunity to tic out. I flail a million times in a row, just to get all of the tension out of my body. Somehow I smack myself in the head with one the charms on my bracelet—probably the conch-shell charm because *wham*—but it's worth it because I feel calmer after.

I text Ezra about what happened. "Should I just leave?" I ask him, even though I don't really mean it—even though my backpack is still slumped on the floor, next to my desk, and my wallet and keys are still in it, and how would I even get home anyway? Hire a ride? That seems extreme.

He doesn't respond, so I text Grandma instead.

She texts back, "Take a deep breath. Is there somewhere private you can go to calm down? Somewhere quite?" She corrects herself: "Quiet. Do you have a meditation app on your glasses? There's an app for everything."

I hide in the bathroom. I don't cry or smooth my hair or look at something on my glasses or anything like that. I just stare at a spot on the wall where the white paint has peeled off and you can see a patch of the old green paint underneath. The patch is shaped like a spatula. It's at armpit level.

I check all the stalls to make sure I'm alone. Then I do the diagonal snapping toe kick at the spatula. Only I kick so softly that my shoe barely goes *whisk* against the wall. I kick it again, only this time, I remember to tilt my head to the right. Then I stop because if I don't, somebody's going to walk in here and see me kicking the wall and call me a defective Loosa again.

I go back to class. I tell myself that when I walk in the door, I'm going to not make eye contact with anybody, and I'm going to head straight to my desk and sit down like this was all a normal bathroom break, and nobody is going to say anything about it, not even Ms. Perez. Everybody will just keep watching the fish movie. And I can put down some random answers for the questions I missed on the worksheet, because who cares, and what does this have to do with biology, and can't I learn more about fish by stocking Grandma's aquarium than watching this grainy, eyebrowy video anyway?

And that's exactly what happens. It's almost like I never started tic-ing and nobody gave me a hard time and I never left the room at all. *Almost.* Because, yeah, we're all watching an animation of what happens when a fish breathes. And yeah, we're writing down that fish breathe through their gills. But also? I'm not thinking about Ruby or Callisto or Grandma's aquarium anymore. I'm thinking about that girl who called me defective, and I'm picturing what could have happened if she'd been in one of those bathroom stalls just now, and what if she up and tried to slap me when she came out and saw me staring at the wall like that? I could have kicked her straight in the chest—using kick number ten, the front thrust heel kick—and sent her stumbling back against the paint spatula. She would have made the wall crumble, and her eyes would have been replaced with two black spirals, and these words would have filled a speech bubble over my head: "*De*fective? More like *e*-ffective." No. That's dumb. "NOW who's defective?" There. That's better.

But here's the thing: nobody's teasing me or yelling at me right now, but nobody's asking if I need help or checking to see if I'm OK either. Sure, nobody cares that I left, but *nobody cares that I left*. I swear, half of life is wishing things won't happen, and the other half is being disappointed when they don't.

# CHAPTER 9

"Absolutely not."

"Come on, Mom. It's not the twenties anymore."

She lets go of the buggy handle and flaps her hands around. "It's *not* the *twen*-ties any-*mooore.*"

"I do *not* sound like that."

"You're staying put. Got it?" I open my mouth to ask why, but before I can say anything, she cuts me off: "I'll tell you why. Three reasons. One: we can't afford private school. Two: virtual school doesn't give you as many opportunities to interact with people. In-person school makes you more well-adjusted socially—"

"Ruby goes to Nobles. That's a virtual school. And *she's* well-adjusted socially."

"How would you know? You've gotten, like, what? One text from this girl?"

Actually, Ruby hasn't texted me at all yet—not even to ask for the cookie recipe—but I don't mention it. I pick up an aquarium bubbler that looks like brain coral and put it down again. "She's well-adjusted."

Mom rolls her eyes. "You sound like your grandma. Anyway, C: there's no hands-on learning in virtual school."

"You mean three."

"What?"

"Three. You said one, two, *C*."

"Well, there you go. Maybe if I hadn't spent all that time in virtual middle school during COVID, I'd be smart enough to remember how to count to three." Uh-oh. *Here* we go. "I missed seeing my friends *so* much during the pandemic. We'd do video chats, but it wasn't the same. Like, you have no idea. *No* idea. And anytime we went anywhere, we had to wear a mask, even if we weren't actually sick."

And there was a shortage of masks.

"There was a shortage of masks at first. Your grandma tried to make me one out of a napkin, a vacuum bag, and two hair elastics."

She laughs. "Eventually she ordered me one from a seamstress, but you couldn't pick the fabric ahead of time. You just got what you got."

Hers had footballs on it.

"Mine had footballs on it."

And there was this piece of wire sewn into it.

"It had this nose piece—this little piece of wire—sewn into the top edge, right here." She points to the bridge of her nose. "And if I didn't squeeze that thing so it fit snugly, my glasses would fog up every time I exhaled. Hey, do you think we need this? Since it's apparently *so* vital to your grandma that we pick up some snails for her tank?" She holds up a bag labeled "Shrimp Feast."

"At least the shrimp might cheer her up—make her forget about her foot for a while," I say. "I don't know why she won't see a doctor about it if it's starting to bother her. You should make her see one."

"And how do you propose I do that?"

"I don't know. Tell her she has to?"

Mom snorts. She hands me the Shrimp Feast. "Do we need this or not?"

I scan the bag with my glasses. Four-and-a-half out of five stars. *These algae pellets make feeding my blue velvet shrimp so easy ... A balanced diet ... I've been using Shrimp Feast for 15 years, and my little shrimpies love it ... !*

"Can't hurt," I say and toss it into the buggy.

Mom says, "But, seriously, you have no idea how happy I was to get back to in-person school. Like, *no* idea. I got to see all my friends again—in real life—and walk in the field with them at recess and talk. I got to play the xylophone. I got to dissect a shark. But the point is, I think it's important that you have experiences like that, too. There are some things you just can't capture online."

"Yeah, well, we are *not* dissecting sharks at school, I'll tell you that much. We're watching *movies* about sharks, which I can totally do online."

"Now, look. Listen. Don't roll your eyes at me. Just listen for one second. If things with these bullies escalate and it gets physical, you can always use your hapkido on them."

"Mom, I've barely—"

"If they're about to hurt you, I want you to do something about it. Understand? But until then, just ignore the haters." I cringe because *haters*. "That's all you've got to do. They call you names? Ignore them—"

"Easier said than—"

"They make fun of your tics? Keep looking at your worksheet or whatever until they get tired of it and quit. They always get tired of it and quit."

"Not *these* people at *this* school. I mean, at my old school, yeah, sure. If somebody was ever mean to me, Lilith or Dora or Ezra would stand up for me, and they'd back down. But not here. Not now. *These* people never let up."

"Never?" Mom says. "Tell me: exactly how many times did anyone at Palma Linda Middle School make fun of you for your tics?"

"You just don't get it. They—"

"I said, how many times did they make fun of you for your tics?"

I pick up a resin skyscraper. It looks like Mera's castle. I add it to the buggy without asking if we can buy it first. Maybe I can re-create Xebel in Grandma's aquarium. "One time."

"One time—"

"But all it took was that one guy back home to call me maestro—*one time*—and you wanted to talk to the principal about it, start a Tourette's-awareness campaign."

"No. No, no, no. It was not a campaign—"

"You wanted an assembly. You wanted a bake sale. I hate to break it to you, Mom, but that's a campaign. That's a campaign."

"Oh, so you *want* me to call your principal. Is that what you're saying?"

"I—"

"You *want* me to organize a bake sale to raise money for the International Parkinson and Movement Disorder Society."

"That's not—"

"Because that's what I'm hearing you say."

"Forget it. Just forget about it. Talking about my tics is making them act up. Let's just go look at the shrimp already."

And Mom's like, "Yeah. That's what I thought."

I'm checking the price of the red cherry shrimp when a text blips onto my lenses. I suck in my breath: it's from Ruby. "Hey! Thanks again for the cookies! I think they're my new favorite. Can you send me the recipe?"

I read and reread her text even though I know there's nothing special about it. *Hey! Thanks again for the cookies!* A red cherry shrimp crawls through a tangle of Christmas moss. *I think they're my new favorite. Can you send me the recipe?* An Amano shrimp—as translucent as glass—shoots across the tank. *Hey! Thanks again for the cookies!*

I'm trying to think of what to say back—something funny but not trying-too-hard funny—when something else appears on my lenses: a red exclamation point and the word "EMERGENCY!"

I can tell the alert is on Mom's glasses, too, because she freezes in the aisle—between the ghost shrimp and the snails—and grips the buggy handle so hard that her knuckles turn white.

*"FIRE. Call 9-1-1? FIRE. Call 9-1-1?"*

A blueprint of a house appears. No, it's too skinny to be a house. It's a mobile home. It's Grandma's mobile home—*our* mobile home. A red dot is blinking in the middle of it. What does that mean? Which smoke detector is that? Which *room* is that? The kitchen? The kitchen. The front and back doors on the blueprint are blinking green arrows: this way to safety.

*"FIRE. Call 9-1-1?"*

Nine: the smell of Play-Doh. The smell of opening a brand-new can of it and seeing that flat, bright, happy surface staring back at you. The smell of possibilities. The smell of your hands after you've rolled the Play-Doh into snakes and forgotten them on the dining room table—at your old house, where absolutely nothing ever caught on fire—and now you're crying because the snakes dried out and when you try to squish them back into the can, they crumble.

One: the smell of Lilith getting too close to the candles on her birthday cake, and her mom saying, "Oh my God!" and Dora saying, "It's over; she's OK," and you saying, "Well, you were just *saying* you wanted to try bangs."

One: the smell of crimping hearts into your ponytail, and your mom asking why you're going to so much trouble for a beach picnic, and you almost saying—but not saying—"Because Ezra will be there."

"It's probably nothing," I say. "Probably a false alarm. You know how sensitive these security devices can be. Always going off for no reason." But if it's probably nothing, why can't I step away from this particular floor tile? Why am I turning my charm bracelet around and around on my wrist? Why am I telling my glasses to call 9-1-1? "It seems like you can't even make pancakes without opening all the windows first, or else the smoke detector will go off. Go off. So, it's probably nothing, really, I'm sure it's nothing."

# CHAPTER 10

The microwave is melted. It looks drippy on the bottom, like it's not really a microwave at all but a very convincing microwave-shaped candle.

It's built into a cabinet over the stove, and that cabinet is burned black. The tiles on the wall behind the stove are so scorched you can't see the acorns painted on them. The stovetop: scorched. The countertop next to it: scorched. Flour and ashes are everywhere. But if you take two steps to the left and stand in front of the sink, or if you take three steps to the right and stand in front of the fridge, everything looks normal. The porcelain frog by the faucet still has a sponge in its mouth. A pizza menu is still stuck to the fridge under a smiling-cactus magnet. It's like the stove and the space around it are in another dimension, and I'm looking through a portal that goes there.

"I don't know what the big deal is," Grandma says from her recliner. "I put it out."

Mom glares at her. "You don't know what the big deal is."

"I put it out."

*"You don't know what the big deal is."*

"It was just a little fire."

"That's like saying it was just a little meteor strike."

"I put it out. I got the bag of flour, and I dumped it over the fire, and I put a lid over it. I put it out."

"Not until you tried to put it out with water, you didn't. And that's the worst thing you can do with a grease fire. No wonder it flared up."

Grandma waves away the damage, like waving away a cloud of gnats. "Merely cosmetic."

"This isn't just cosmetic, Mom. This is … it's … just *look at this*. I don't know how you didn't get burned. Here, let me see your arms."

"Oh, stop it, Bella. I'm fine." But Grandma holds out her arms anyway.

Mom examines them. "Good Lord, Mom, your arm hairs are singed. Look at that. Singed clean off. Right there. And there. See? I'll tell you what: your guardian angel must have been working overtime today. You could have died. I mean, you could have *died*."

Grandma puts her hand over her heart, like she's doing the Pledge of Allegiance. "I regret that I have but one life to give for my home fries."

"Oh, stop it." Mom takes the sponge out of the ceramic frog's mouth, wets it at the sink, and tries to wipe down the stovetop, but in an exhausted way, like she doesn't really mean it, like she knows it's pointless. After just a few seconds, she gives up and slings the sponge into the sink. She finds a spoon in the dishwasher, opens the freezer, and gets a carton of Crick-or-Treat from her new stockpile. It's a seasonal flavor, so she always buys a ton of it when it hits the freezer aisle in September. She sits on the ashy, floury floor—right in front of the oven—takes the lid off the carton, and flings it Frisbee-style across the room. Then she digs in.

I wonder if it smelled like ones in here— like burning hair—when the fire was still going. Or if it smelled more like twos: fried food. I mean, *now* it doesn't smell like either of those things. *Now* it just smells like smoke—like a campfire, but in a bad way. If Grandma was making home fries, though ...

Grandma gets her phone and hobbles to the kitchen with us. She says each word as she types it: "What. To. Do. After. A. Grease. Fire. In. The. Kitchen." She taps the screen theatrically. "It says to turn off the air-conditioning."

Mom looks at her like *what?*

Grandma holds up her phone. "It says to turn off the air-conditioning. I don't know. I didn't write it."

Mom groans. "I'm texting Sophia."

My adrenaline surges. That's Ezra's mama.

"First it says to turn off the air conditioning. Then it says to open the windows and turn on a ceiling fan." Grandma looks up, as if to confirm that no, we do not, in fact, have a ceiling fan in the kitchen she's owned since before I was born.

"I'm pretty sure she and Livvy"—that's Ezra's mom—"have done this kind of ... oh, I don't know, *restoration* work before. Whatever you'd call it."

Grandma tells me to turn on the ceiling fan in the living room. "And open all the windows, too. You know how to open them, don't you?"

"Yeah. I mean, I think so."

"Just turn the little thingies on top first." She acts it out for me. "You know. The little thingies."

As I leave the kitchen, she says, "Next, use vinegar—"

"Mom, this is getting ridiculous. Don't worry about it, OK? Just leave it be. Go sit down. You should probably stay off that foot."

"—to clean up soot and grease."

"Good Lord."

"Do we have any white vinegar? Would balsamic vinegar work, do y'all think? It's going to smell like a salad bar in here." She takes a few steps toward the pantry before she stops and winces.

"I told you to *sit down*."

Windows open, fan clicking rhythmically, I go back to the kitchen.

Did you know that you can look up the history of a smoke detector? It's easy. Just look at it, and when the smoke-detector menu shows up on your glasses, go to History, and they'll show you every time it's gone off: the date it went off, how long it went off, whether or not you told it to call the fire department because it went off.

Grandma got this smoke detector about a year ago. That's in the history, too. Guess how many times the alarm has gone off since then? Go ahead. Guess.

Higher.

Higher.

Nope. Not even close.

# CHAPTER 11

Ezra asks why I don't just tell Grandma she's not allowed to cook anymore.

"Yeah, great idea. While we're at it, let's tell all the criminals they're not allowed to go out crime-ing anymore. That'll stop them."

"OK, OK. So, what about getting her a new oven? It sounds like she's got a dumb one. With a normal oven, you can control it from your glasses."

"I know how ovens work."

"You could lock her out of using it when you're not home. Lydia's grandma got a new oven, and she loves it."

I feel like I just swallowed an ice chip. "Oh. Really."

"Don't be that way."

"What way? I'm not being any way." I press the starfish charm on my bracelet against my wrist, where my pulse is. When I take it away, there's a star-shaped indentation in my skin.

"I was telling her that my moms and I are going to visit you and fix your kitchen, that's all. And she told me about her grandma's new oven. See?"

*Ping!* There's a picture of Lydia and her grandma posing in front of the oven, doing *look at this!* hands at a pan of scones.

Lydia's wearing her peapod earrings again.

"She said her grandma was forgetting to turn the old oven off, too. Either that or her grandma would be out somewhere, and she'd think, 'Oh my gosh! Did I leave the oven on?' One time her grandma was at the hairdresser's when it happened—in the middle of getting her hair colored—so she couldn't even go straight home to check. She had to wait till the whole job was done first. And according to Lydia, it took especially long because there were highlights involved, which I guess are complicated? Her grandma couldn't even relax and enjoy herself during her $600 pampering session or whatever. She was *that* nervous. Convinced her whole house was in flames." Did it ever occur to Ezra that this story about Lydia's grandma is like an ad you can't skip before a video? "She finally got herself a new oven because she was sick of the worry. And now, wherever she is, she can pull up the oven app and turn it off if she needs to. So can Lydia and her mom. They have the app, too."

"I *said* I know how an oven works."

"Fine, geez, I'm just trying to help."

I never want to see Lydia's peapod earrings again.

"*OK, Glazier,*" I say. "*Clear my lenses.*"

My glasses point me to a pharmacy where I can buy lens wipes for nine bucks. *My vision is so much clearer when I use these! ... No streaks! No Lint! WOW! ...*

Oh, forget it.

I wave my hand to clear my lenses. I should have done that to begin with.

But as soon as all the screens disappear, one final screen shows up: an ad for a silver peapod charm that would match the other charms on my bracelet "like peas in a pod."

I tell Ezra I've got to go because Grandma's calling me, even though she isn't. I flop back on my bed and stare at the ceiling. There's a beige spot where water leaked in at some point. I realize I don't remember what my ceiling looked like in my old room. I'm almost positive it was smooth and white—the color of soy milk—but the more I think about it, the more I'm not sure. I don't understand it: how could I see my bedroom ceiling every day for 10 years and forget what it looks like after less than a month away? Was I daydreaming too much when I looked at it? Was I too busy imagining what Callisto would look like if she were a human, or what I would look like if I were a fish, or what we would both look like if we were mermaids? Was I too busy recalling every time Ezra had laughed at one of my jokes or lent me one of his pencils, and trying to figure out if he *like*-liked me? Or playing back every time I said something stupid in front of him and cringing over it—the way I keep thinking about asking Ruby to "confirm her number for me" now?

I sit up.

I don't *like*-like Ruby. Do I? I'm already in a relationship with someone who says I'm, like, his girl—someone who is willing to have a long-distance relationship with me and everything—so *like*-liking a whole other person right now would just be stupid. Besides, I probably don't want to *be with* her. I probably just want to *be* her. I admire her, and I want to be her friend. That's all this is.

I start to text her: "Sorry I forgot to tell you the recipe."

No. That's not true. I didn't actually *forget* anything. *Delete.*

"Sorry I haven't asked my mom for the recipe yet."

What am I apologizing for? It's just a recipe. And she may not even want it really. She may just be acting polite. *Delete.*

"I have good news and bad news. The good news is my mom knows the recipe. The bad news is my kitchen caught fire."

*Delete.*

I go to the kitchen. I eat a lot of cheese. I peek into the living room—over the flour-smeared counter—and stare at the play-through Grandma's watching. A sheriff is having a shootout on top of a moving train. Only, wait. I don't think Grandma's watching it at all. I think she's sleeping in her recliner.

I step closer. Yeah. She fell asleep with her hand in a bag of Doritos, even though it's not even dark out yet. Her footrest is still up, so I can see the red spot on the bottom of her foot. It's bigger and darker now, or maybe I'm imagining things.

Mom's sitting on the couch, folding the heap of laundry that's been sitting there for who knows how long. When the sheriff in the play-through swaps out his six-shooter for a sawed-off shotgun and starts shooting at the bad guys like *KAPOW KAPOW*, Mom rolls her eyes and turns the channel to some old movie where a bunch of women are yakking in a beauty salon.

"Hey," I half-whisper to her. I point at Grandma's foot and shrug.

Mom half-whispers back, "She doesn't care. And I can't make her care. Here. Watch this."

She shakes Grandma's shoulder to wake her up.

Grandma shifts in her chair. She opens her eyes.

"Mom! Your foot's looking bad."

Grandma says, "No, thank you, baby, I'm full," and closes her eyes again.

"Mom, your *foot*. It's looking bad. You want me to call a doctor?"

Grandma blinks. "Why?"

"For your foot."

Grandma shakes her head.

"We can do it over the phone," Mom tells her. "It's easy. You may not even need to go anywhere unless they need an X-ray."

"I don't need a doctor."

"I think it's infected."

"I'm just going to keep off it for a while. Keep it elevated."

"It's infected. Mom. *Mom.*" Grandma's asleep again—or pretending to be.

Mom looks at me like, *see?*

I ask her for the cookie recipe, and while she finds it on her glasses, I get out the pH test kit from the shelf under the fish tank. I fill a vial with aquarium water and add four drops of a chemical to it. The water sample turns baby-blanket blue. That means the pH is safe. I rinse out the vial and put everything away, and I'm being kind of loud, right? Like, the vials are clinking together, and the little bottles of chemicals are rattling around. But Grandma sleeps through all of it.

Back in my room, I look closer at Grandma's barrel-racing trophy. On top, a bronze cowgirl is riding a bronze horse around a bronze barrel. On the side, a bronze plaque says, "Ladies' Barrel Racing. Third Place. 1998." That's it. It doesn't say the name of the rodeo—I'm assuming rodeos have names—or tell you where it happened.

When I tell Glazier to look for videos of Sarah Kowalski in a rodeo in 1998, I don't think anything will turn up. I mean, that was the twentieth century. Did people record videos with their glasses—I mean, their phones—back then? Did they even have phones? Like, *phone*-phones?

But then a black horse with a white spot between its eyes is flying across my lenses, and these weird, *wah-wah* trumpets are blaring a circus-tent song, and an announcer is shouting, *"SHE'S NOT JUST ALONG FOR THE RIDE!"* and a woman with a number eight—*cinnamon*—pinned to the back of her shirt is smacking the horse with a rope, and her long, brown hair is streaming behind her, and oh my God, that woman is my grandma. Because even though the footage is grainy, and even though the brim of her black cowboy hat is casting a shadow over her face, there's just something about her that's so *Grandma*. Maybe it's the way her jaw is shaped. Maybe it's the way she leans forward in the saddle, or the way she bends her arm when she's pulling on the reins. I don't know. But once I recognize it's her, it's *her*.

So after I send Ruby the recipe, I send her the rodeo video. I text, "This is my grandma! You met her the other day. This was her 52 years ago!"

I'm still sitting there on my bed, worrying that two exclamation points in a single text make me sound crazy, when Ruby writes back: "Your grandma looks like a superhero!"

# CHAPTER 12

"Your grandma looks like a witch."

Ruby laughs. "Well, my grandma says that in the '90s, every girl was a witch for at least five minutes. So, I guess you're not wrong."

She starts to take back the picture she'd placed in my hand just a minute ago, but I hold it tight against my chest so she can't grab it.

"Wait, wait!" I say. "That didn't come out right. I mean it in a *good* way." But, hold on: I feel like I've lived this moment before. Only, I couldn't have. *Could* I? Have Ruby and I talked about her grandma before? About the '90s? No. No, we haven't. Of course, we haven't. So why do I feel this way? I try to ignore the déjà vu that's strangling me like some monstrous kudzu vine.

I look at the picture again. The girl staring back at me is wearing reddish-black lipstick, smudged eyeliner, and a black choker with a silver pentagram hanging from it. Her black hair is parted in a zigzag. She's staring into the camera like *I dare you.*

And finally I'm like, "I love this look. I wish *I* could pull off this look."

"You could *totally* pull off a goth look," Ruby says. She frames my face with her hands. "Don't get me wrong: the whole girl-next-door thing you have going on right now is super flattering. Really. But with a little black eye shadow—"

"No."

"Or ... *oh!* Have you ever considered a grassmetal look? Do you have any leather overalls?"

"No!"

She laughs. "I'm kidding. Well, mostly. But turn the picture over. Look at the back."

Somebody wrote "1998—Juárez?" on it with a blue ballpoint pen.

I run my finger over the writing. "Who was Juárez?"

"Not who—*where.* It's a city in Mexico, just over the border. Grandma was born in El Paso, so Juárez was, like, *right* there. And she says you could just, like, *walk* there, and you didn't have to show any ID or anything. Crazy, huh?"

"*Your* grandma was from Texas? No way! So was mine!"

"No way."

"Yeah! Near Beaumont. It's on the Louisiana side." I almost blurt out that that's a sign Ruby and I were meant to be friends, but I manage to keep it in. Instead I say, "Imagine taking pictures and not being able to see them until you print them out. What if they turned out bad? You couldn't just delete them."

Ruby shrugs. "You'd have to throw them away, I guess. But think of all the toner you'd be wasting."

"And who wants to mess with printers anyway? They're so—*Oof!*" Somebody bumps into my chair. It's a little kid with a green belt who's waving his hands in front of his face and gazing into the distance, playing a game on his glasses. Meanwhile, this *other* kid—this yellow belt—is clucking like a rooster and going "ba-*kock*" to distract him.

Ruby gets onto him: "Geez, Micah. Pay attention."

He sighs. "OK."

"Master Avery would remind you about the three *A*s of personal protection."

"O-*kay!*"

"Which are?"

He sighs again. "Aware, alert, and avoid."

"Excellent." She holds up her hand for a high-five, and Micah gives her one. He pretends he's doing it reluctantly—like he's mad at her—but he's fighting a smile. I can tell that, in reality, he looks up to her.

I can't be *too* annoyed at Micah for running into me because the front room is already swirling with students. There's a rainbow of belt colors. Old people, young people, ambiguously aged people who look old and young at the same time.

A blue belt who's about my age is taking off her hoop earrings. She puts them in the leather purse that's hanging from the back of her wheelchair and has a pattern of ivy stamped onto it. That makes Ruby say, "Oh! Charlotte!

Thanks for reminding me!" and run over to the front desk, where she asks a worker for two band-aids.

She's putting the second band-aid over her earring when a pregnant woman with a brown belt tied under her huge belly walks into the big mat room. I don't know if that's some kind of signal or what, but next thing I know, everyone is rushing to get their shoes off and cram through the doorway. Ruby takes back the picture of her grandma real fast and tucks it into her NASA backpack. She and I scurry into the big mat room, put our shoes on the rack, and claim hooks for her backpack and my purse.

We all line up on the edge of the mat, in order of rank, facing the mirrors. I'm the next-to-last one in line. The only person who comes after me is Micah, who probably still sleeps in a racecar bed.

Ruby is at the other end of the room, with just the pregnant woman in front of her.

During warmups, we roll our shoulders and touch our toes and stretch, stretch, stretch, and while everyone else counts off 20 jumping jacks, Charlotte does just the arm-motion part and counts along with us. And while we all do 10 push-ups, Charlotte holds onto her armrests and lifts herself up in her chair. And I realize I'm staring at her, which makes me feel *super* bad because sometimes people stare at me when my tics act up, and it's basically the worst feeling ever. So I look at my reflection instead.

I can't actually *do* 10 push-ups. I do four, and then I just lie there while Master Avery says, "Come on, Louisa! Go, go, go!"

Then warmups are over, and Master Avery says we're going to be working in pairs, and I'm like please don't make us pick our own partners—please, please, please—because what if Ruby doesn't pick me, and what if *no one* picks me, and what if I have to stand by myself until Master Avery says she'll be my partner out of pity, and why did Mom have to sign me up for this? Why? Why couldn't she sign me up for something more relaxing? Like arson class. Or DIY orthodontics.

Luckily Master Avery is picking our partners for us. "Kaya, you're with Charlotte. Micah and Kendrick, you're together, but if I see any funny business ..." She gives them a look. "Ruby, you're with Louisa."

I follow her to the middle of the mat, where she stakes out a spot for us. She bows, I bow. She opens her mouth to say something, but Master Avery doesn't waste any time. She tells us to take turns kicking at each other's chins—higher belt rank goes first—except for Charlotte, who is supposed to work on blocking the other person's kicks instead. And there's no way I can ask Ruby anything when her foot is flying at my face or I'm struggling to get my foot even as high as her chest.

Ruby says I'm doing great. I'm not.

"Thanks. Your leg is good." Oh, God. "I mean, your kick is good. And your leg gets really, you know, high."

Ruby laughs. "Your leg is good, too. So, hey: did you get your grandma's aquarium up and running?"

"Yeah, it's a lot better than it was before we moved in with her. Because ... well, I think it can be hard for her to remember to do things. I syphoned out most of the old water that was in there, which was pretty gross because I had to use my mouth on the syphon. It's like this: imagine you're drinking a milkshake with a straw, only you're supposed to stop it before it actually reaches your mouth—and the milkshake is made with the mysterious, brown liquid that collects at the bottom of your crisper drawer."

"*Blech!*"

"Exactly. So, that was bad enough, right? But the thing with aquariums—or, aquaria or whatever—is that for them to succeed, everything has to be right. For them to fail, just one thing has to be wrong. It can be water that's too warm, or water that's too cool. It can be a pH that's too high, or too low. Maybe you accidentally overfeed the fish. Or maybe you don't change out the water frequently enough. Or maybe you do change it frequently enough, but you replace too much water at once. That's what I'm worried *I* did. Because if you change too much of an aquarium's water, you can throw everything out of balance and restart the nitrogen cycle—Sorry. This is boring, isn't it?"

"No!"

"I'm shutting up now. I promise."

"No! OK, see? Here's the thing: I can *totally* out-bore you. Because you just reminded me of what the Martian bio-mining team is dealing with down in Chile, and I have two words for you: *Anabaena cylindrica*."

I laugh. "Wow. You win."

"Told you."

"But, like, seriously: what is *Ana*—? *Ana*—? *Anaconda Cinderella*?"

Master Avery claps her hands. "OK, OK," says. "What's missing?"

Everyone but me answers, *"Kiyups,"* in unison. I look around in wonder. This is a cult, right? Definitely a cult.

Master Avery tilts her head at me. "Louisa, did we go over what *kiyups* are? We *didn't*? I can't believe I forgot that. Bad, Master Avery! Bad!" She jokingly slaps herself on the back of the hand. "Everyone? This is Louisa. She moved here from the Saint Petersburg area, and this is her first group class."

"Did Hurricane *Louisa* make *Louisa* move here?" Micah asks. "That's crazy." He looks at me. "Isn't that crazy?"

Ruby pipes up: "Yeah, OK, Micah. Like she's never heard *that* one before."

"What? I'm just asking."

"OK, OK," says Master Avery, "back on track everybody. A *kiyup* is a sound we make when we kick or strike somebody. It doesn't sound like *hi-yah*, like when people do karate on a show. It sounds like this." She half-growls, half-yells. It's a werewolf sound that makes me jump. "Your back teeth have to touch when you *kiyup*," she says. "You have to open your lips, almost like you're smiling, but your molars should still touch."

And I'm not sure what she says after that because I get that dripping-candle-wax sensation that means my tampon has chosen this exact moment to give up the ghost. And you know what? Maybe I'm wrong. Maybe it's, I don't know, sweat. Because we *were* doing all those kicks, and *drip*, no. No, no. This is not sweat.

Master Avery is going on and on: "There's a saying: 'The first one to laugh in training is the first one to cry in battle.' That's why we need to take this seriously. That's why we need to *kiyup.* That's why we need to be martial. Now, we talk a lot about being martial in here, don't we? But does anyone know what it means to be martial? Any guesses? What does it *mean* to be martial?"

*Drip.*

"Really? No one? Not *one* person can tell me what 'martial' means? I find that hard to believe."

*Drip, drip.*

I raise my hand.

Master Avery flashes me a warm, "have a sugar cookie" smile. "Louisa! I'd love your input on this. New students mean new ideas, new perspectives. What does 'martial' mean to you?"

"I need to use the restroom."

Micah snickers. Master Avery and Ruby *sssh* him at the same time.

"I mean, I need to use the restroom, *ma'am.* I wasn't raising my hand to answer the question, ma'am. It was bad timing." Oh, no. "It was bad timing." I almost flail my arms, but I try to turn it into an awkward, casual-looking, arm-foldy thing at the last second.

What's wrong with me? Why am I like this? I mean, duh, I know why I'm like this— Tourette's is why I'm like this—but like why am *I* like this*?* It's not fair. Why do *I* have to have this embarrassing condition while there's some baby-elephant poacher out there who's walking around all tic-free, like *lah-dee-dah.*

Master Avery waves me to the bathroom. I walk as fast as I can without jogging. When I bow at the edge of the mat, it's more like a quick nod *yes.* During my almost-jog, I think I hear somebody whispering my name, like they're talking about me. And I'm *this* close to crying, even though I probably misheard them—because all I could *really* hear was my heartbeat in my ears and the *tsh-tsh* sound my feet made against the mat. I must have misheard. I must have.

When I get to the bathroom, I close the door so hard that the wooden-stars decoration hanging on it goes *bam.* My belt comes off easily enough—turns out, it was halfway untied already—and slipping off the top half of my uniform is no big deal, but to get my pants off, I have to pick at the knot with my fingernails, and just when I start to worry I'll have to ask someone for scissors so I can cut the drawstring, the knot loosens. I hold my breath as I check out the damage: a quarter-sized splotch of blood on my underwear, two Tylenol-sized ones on the inside of my pants, and just a pin-prick-sized one on the outside. OK. OK. I can work with this.

I wrap the crime-scene-looking tampon in 1,000 layers of toilet paper and hide it under a bunch of paper towels that are already in the trash. I unspool more toilet paper from the roll, fold it like an accordion, stuff it into my underwear, and wish it wasn't this cheap, half-see-through kind that schools and stores and restaurants and charging stations and probably prisons always use.

I tug the hem of my T-shirt down as low as I can get it, pull my pants back up, and knot them again, only not as tight this time because I'm not making *that* mistake again. I turn my back to the mirror over the sink, stand on my tiptoes, and look over my shoulder. You can only see the blood if you're looking right at it, and only if I bend over in a ridiculous way that I would never do in real life.

And I'm feeling pretty good about it—all things considered—except that after I wash my hands, put on the rest of my uniform, and walk back into the mat room, everyone is wrestling, and it looks like violent yoga, and half of the students have their butts in the air as they pin the other half to the mat. Even Charlotte is doing it. She's out of her wheelchair and pinning a mohawked guy—my mom's age—to the ground with just her arms.

So much for not bending over.

Ruby tells me the hold is called *ka-*something *yoko* something. I'm too distracted to pay attention. We sit cross-legged on the mat and watch another pair of people flip each other over and take turns practicing the hold. Ruby points out little things the hold-er is doing to the hold-ee: keep your hips low, keep your head down, get your knee into their armpit.

"Want to try it?" she asks me.

"Why don't you go first?" I want to keep my back to the mat as long as possible. Also: this is some        meerkats-wrestling-in-the-desert awkwardness. "What do I have to do?"

"Just lie there. Act like you're dead, basically."

Dead of embarrassment, maybe. "Sounds good."

After I lie down and she pins me, and her hands are clasped behind my neck, I notice the spice-racky smell of her soap or her perfume or her laundry detergent. It's *almost* the smell of the Middle Eastern grocery store where Mom buys her spices in bulk—where they also sell incense and prayer beads and little pistachio candies—but not quite.

Ruby readjusts her hands. Her fingers graze the back of my neck, and a shiver runs from my spine—between my shoulder blades—down both of my arms. She weighs down on me, pressing me into the mat like a cookie cutter pressing into rolled-out dough, and I worry that she'll be able to feel my heart beating faster through my uniform, and why is my heart beating faster anyway? What's *its* problem?

Of course, I'm also worrying that the wisp of toilet paper in my underwear isn't going to get me through all this being-pressed business. So I do what I have to do. I ignore the embarrassed, ate-too-much-*queso* feeling in my stomach and tell Ruby I need a tampon. I whisper it, right into her face, which is conveniently close to mine, so close that I can see the peacock-feather-green eyeliner she's wearing today.

She gasps.

I nod. "Yep."

"Uh-oh."

"Yep."

"Are you sure? I mean, of course, you're sure. Sorry. So, anyway. Yeah. Tampons. Did you look under the sink? Because you should look under the sink. Master Avery keeps, like, *supplies* there. Go back and check, and if there aren't any, just look in the little pocket of my backpack. The inside one, you know what I mean? I'm 90% sure—no, 85% sure—I've got one in there. 87% sure."

"Oh my God, thank you. Like, *thank you*."

"No problem. We've all been there. Like, even Master Avery has been there. I mean, she hasn't *said* she's been there, but come on, she's been doing this longer than I've been alive, and *white pants.*"

"*White! Pants!*"

Ruby lets me up. My rib cage stops feeling like a crab claw that's being cracked open at a seafood restaurant. "It happened to me at our Samhain party last year," she says. "You know, *this* did."

I say, "Oh, no! Really?" like I know what Samhain is.

"Yeah, and I was wearing this white, floofy skirt." She shakes her head. "But, sorry. I shouldn't keep you. Go to the bathroom. Go." She waves her hand in the air to get Master Avery's attention. Then she points at me and at the bathroom.

For a second I worry Master Avery is going to get onto me for going to the bathroom twice in five minutes, but all that happens is she nods at me, turns back to the mohawked guy, and says, "Switch your feet. Yeah, like that."

Under the sink, there's a pack of Clorox wipes, a spray bottle of Windex, bundles of graham-cracker-colored paper towels, stacks of toilet paper rolls—and a box each of tampons and pads. There's also a box of laundry-detergent pens.

Ruby's right. Master Avery has totally been there.

# CHAPTER 13

Ezra points at something in the aquarium. "What is that?"

The new microwave plays "Twinkle, Twinkle" instead of beeping three times, like the old one did. I open it and take out two hot mugs of something Mom calls "hot-chocolate cake." Mom's busy hauling lumber outside, so I sneak a pint of her Crick-or-Treat out of the freezer. "What is what?" I ask Ezra.

"That green stuff."

"The green stuff is java moss."

He shakes his head. "I don't think this is moss."

I blow the sawdust off a tray, set the mugs, ice cream, and two spoons on it, and walk over to the tank. There's a smear of dark-green gunk on the inside of the glass. "Oh." I frown. "It's algae."

"Is it supposed to be there?"

"It's no big deal." It's not, is it? "I'll deal with it. Come on."

We're on our way to my room when Mom calls after me to leave my door open. I can barely hear her because she's on the deck and the circular saw is so loud.

"I know, I know."

"What?"

"I said, *I know.*"

So I *almost* shut the door behind us, but not quite. Ezra sets his backpack on my spinny desk chair. For some reason, his backpack rattles. What does he have in there? Vitamins? Maracas?

You know, come to think of it, I helped him pick out that backpack. Which shade of red did I like better: chili pepper or fire hydrant? (Chili pepper.) One water-bottle holder or two? (Doesn't matter.) Solar fabric and a charging pocket? (Yes, obviously.) It's weird to see something from the Before Time here in my bedroom right now. It's like seeing someone dressed in old-timey, Conestoga-wagon clothes trying out new glasses at an electronics store.

Ezra says he has a surprise for me. He opens his backpack and takes out a stuffed moose that hangs from a white, plastic clip. Its antlers are made out of a different kind of fabric: purple velvet, blue denim, red corduroy. When Ezra shakes the moose, it rattles. When he squeezes it, it makes a crinkly sound like folding down the bag inside a cereal box.

"It's the moose rattle you had when you were a baby!" he says. "Well, it's *just like* the one you had as a baby, anyway. Like the one you had hanging on your closet door back home, remember?"

"Oh."

"I know it was bothering you that you didn't take it with you, so I did a little searching"—he gestures to his glasses—"and found this."

I put the tray down on the bed. "That's so nice of you."

"When I mentioned to the seller that I wasn't buying it for a baby, he seemed really confused at first."

"Very, very nice of you."

"But I explained the whole situation to him, and get this: he didn't even make me pay for shipping."

"But it was a peacock."

"He—What?"

"It was a peacock rattle. Not a moose rattle. But hey! No, no. Don't look at me like that. I still love it, OK? I think it's adorable. And it still sounds exactly the same as the peacock." I give it a shake and look straight into its black, velvet eyes.

I hang the moose on my new closet doorknob. I open and close the door. The moose rattles and makes the same soft *thump* that the peacock always did. My stomach sinks. My throat gets tight. I sit on the bed and take a bite of quote-unquote "cake" to keep from crying. I chew once.

Ezra laughs. "That bad?"

I chew again, slowly. I force myself to swallow. "I'm so glad we're going to have an oven again. You have no idea."

Ezra takes a bite of his cake. He shrugs and keeps eating it. His spoon clinks against the mug. "Honestly, it's fine."

While the circular saw goes *reeeee* and the nail gun goes *blam* and Ezra's moms yell to each other for more nails or wood, Ezra and I look at his latest drawings, which he pulls out of a folder and spreads across my desk. This might be the first time I've used this desk for a desky purpose. Usually it's just a place for me to store my comics and display my figurines.

Most of Ezra's drawings are colored-pencil sketches of his Shaman character summoning a spirit—a levitating spirit with curly, blonde hair that's floating around her face. In some versions, the hair is a blonde splash of water. In other versions, it's blonde snakes.

In one picture, the spirit is attacking the Shaman—kicking him. I point to her foot. "This isn't right."

"What do you mean?" Ezra picks up the drawing and squints at it.

"This is a roundhouse kick. The way this spirit—is she a spirit?—is drawn now, she's about to hit the Shaman with the top of her foot. But we were working on that kick last week, and Master Avery says you can hurt your foot that way. She needs to pull her toes back and hit the Shaman with the ball of her foot."

"What do you mean, 'pull her toes back'?"

"Like ... like this. Stand here." I position him so that he's standing in front of me, but in profile. I hold onto the side of the bed so I don't fall over, and I do a slow, careful roundhouse kick at him. The ball of my foot comes to rest against his chest. "See my toes? You need to make them like that."

Then I do the kick for real, and I swear to God, I barely touch him, but he's like, "Hey! That hurts."

I tell him I'm sorry even though, like I said before, I barely touched him. I hug him, and I realize it's the first time I've hugged him since before the hurricane. He smells like the same orangey pomade he's used for years. He's so sturdy somehow. It's like hugging one of those big trees out in California that's older than ... well, California.

He hugs me back. I feel floaty, like I took a dose of Benadryl and it just kicked in.

"Hey," he says, "do you know how to escape this?" He hugs me tighter.

"The question is, do I *want* to?"

"Well, do you?" He loosens his grip, like he's about to step away. "Hey, sorry. I should have asked first. It's just that I don't know when I'll see you again after Mom and Mama get the kitchen patched up and we leave. But, still, I shouldn't have—"

But I lean into him. "It's fine." Then I remember the not-technically-closed bedroom door. I have visions of my mom throwing it open. Or, even more embarrassing: one of Ezra's moms. "Well, maybe I know how to escape it," I say against his shoulder. "There's this one move. But we've only practiced it a few times, and I am not any good at it yet."

"Try it."

"I'm telling you: I've only done it, like, twice."

He laughs. "Just do it. You're kind of cute when you do aikido."

"Hapkido."

"What?"

"It's hapkido. Aikido is a whole other thing. From what Master Avery has said, there are a lot of similarities, though. Lots of joint locks and throws and—"

"OK, OK, just do it."

I *kiyup* and tap both his kidneys with the sides of my hands. I use that tiny bone that's just above your wrist—the pisiform bone. It's as round and hard as a glass marble.

Ezra sucks in his breath.

I'm like, "Are you OK?"

And he's like, "Do I look OK? No! No, I'm not OK."

"I'm sorry."

He steps away from me and rubs his lower back. "What's the matter with you?"

"I'm sorry, I'm sorry. It was ... a tic."

"Oh, *sure*. I'm—" Then he looks at the door, and so do I because someone's walking this way. We jump back from each other. Now there are four feet between us, and my hands are in my pockets, and his thumbs are hitched under his suspenders, and he is literally whistling. Yeah. *Real* casual.

Grandma opens my door. Her eyes are as empty as a roadside motel with a burned-out *vacancy* sign and a parking lot full of trash. She glances at the drawings on my desk. She glances at the tray on my bed. Then she looks at me. "I can't find my toothbrush, Bella."

*Bella.*

One time Dora and I went to this swimming hole where you can rent innertubes to float around in. Somehow I slipped through the center of mine into the cold water, and my feet touched the slimy bottom, and water burned my nose, and for a second—before I clamored back up—my brain was icy with panic.

This moment feels like *that* moment.

*I can't find my toothbrush, Bella.*

"It must be in the bathroom, where it always is, *Grandma*." I hope when she hears "Grandma," her dementia fog will clear for a minute. "You know, in the holder? By the sink?"

"Don't be stupid," she says. "I don't mean that one. I mean the other one."

"The ... other one?"

She glares at me. She doesn't look like herself anymore. But she doesn't look *unlike* herself either. She looks like someone wearing a rubber Grandma mask they got from the Halloween store. "Stupid," she says. She stomps to the stack of jigsaw puzzles and shoves them aside. Behind them is a PlayStation box that is way too light to hold an actual PlayStation. She opens it and takes things out, dropping them on the floor: an old pair of glasses, a handful of receipts, a ticket stub from a Clint Black concert, a second-place ribbon from some rodeo, a single white button in a tiny zip-top bag.

"Grandma, if you—"

"*Stupid!*"

"If you tell me what the toothbrush looks like, I can help you look for it. Like, what color is it?" I pretend to look for a toothbrush under my pillow, under my bed, under my rug. I use my eyes to text Ezra to look for the toothbrush, too, but he just stands there, staring at Grandma, with his mouth hanging open.

"LOOK FOR IT!!!" I text again. Bubbly-toothbrushing emoji.

"It's electric," Grandma says. "White and electric. With, like, a ... you know." She pantomimes pressing a button with her thumb.

"Right," I say. "Ezra, check the ... I don't know, the printer."

He looks around like *what printer?*

And I'm like, "The 2-D printer. The black thing, over there." He doesn't move. "Oh, never mind." I look in the paper tray. I look behind the door where the ink goes. I look in the paper tray again. "I don't see it here, Grandma. Check the bathroom again."

She goes to my desk and starts picking up my figurines, one at a time, and putting them down: Mera, Aquaman, Saturn Girl, Black Canary.

"Don't ... look, be careful with that, OK?" I say when she messes with the fringe on Black Canary's jacket. "What do you need an electric toothbrush for anyway?"

"I need to clean the fish tank. There's green stuff on the glass."

"I know. Ezra told me about it. But you can't use an electric toothbrush to clean it off. You'll electrocute yourself. Just wait till this evening, and I'll deal with it."

But she's not listening to me. She's looking at Ezra's drawings on the desk and moving them around. She picks up the one where the spirit has snakes for hair. She smiles. "Can I have this?"

"You hate snakes," I remind her.

"These aren't snakes," she says. "They're eels."

"I'm pretty sure they're snakes," I say. "Ezra, aren't they—"

"I've been wanting to get some eels for my tank. You can buy them at the pet store, you know—these itty-bitty eels. They move under the gravel like ..." She slithers her arm in the air. "Real cute. So, can I have this drawing, or not?"

I look at Ezra.

"Sure," he says. "It's yours. I ... I'm going to go help my moms for a while."

"Wait," I say. "You can—"

"No, I should really help them. I promised I'd … yeah."

He leaves while Grandma looks at the rest of his drawings. "Come see these," she says to me. "Aren't these great? Really. Come look."

I look at the drawings I've already looked at and I realize that the blonde, curly-haired spirit looks familiar. The compositions are all so clean. They look the way sashimi tastes. Ezra isn't trying to cram a lot of action into a little frame, the way he usually does. There's a lot of white space surrounding the Shaman and this spirit. They live in a minimalist world. There's no clutter. No distractions.

My heart stops.

It's Lydia.

# CHAPTER 14

My tics are like the weather. When they're mild—like a sunny day with a light breeze—I can forget I even have them. When they're severe—like a thunderstorm with hail—I'll fling my arms until they're tired or repeat words for hours.

Not getting enough sleep makes my tics worse. Stress and PMS make them worse, too.

My meds make them kind of better. And so does exercise. And so does TMS, which stands for trans-*something* magnetic stimulation. I can never remember the first word.

When I get a TMS treatment, the first thing my doctor does is wheel this big machine into the room. Then she extends this arm from the machine. There's a hat-like thing at the end of the arm. It's like one of those old-fashioned hair dryers you see women sitting under in old movies. The doctor puts the hat on me, tightens the strap under my chin, and pushes some buttons on the machine. That's how the hat starts to, like, magnetize my brain. Which *sounds* like it would hurt—having your brain magnetized—but it doesn't feel like anything.

The doctor leaves the hat on me for half an hour while she dims the lights and plays some music that's supposed to be relaxing but has a babbling brook in the background and just makes me want to pee.

I tell Grandma all of this in her own doctor's exam room, but when I'm done describing the process, she just says, "When are we getting out of here?" She picks her purse up off the floor and plops it in her lap. "I'm only here so we can go to the pet store later. Remember that."

"We can't leave yet, Mom. We have to do your TMS first," Mom said.

"It doesn't work. It's a scam."

"It's not a scam. It'll help you have more good days and fewer bad days."

Grandma unzips her purse, takes out her phone, and starts playing a chiming, plinking match-three game. It has a pirate theme. When she makes a move, a voice bellows, "Shiver me timbers!" or "Blimey!"

"Any day I'm still breathing is a good day," Grandma mumbles.

I pat her on the arm. "I can't believe I'm saying this, but: Mom's right. My tics used to be *so* much worse before I started TMS."

Grandma snickers. "You sound like a commercial. *Side effects of TMS may include constipation, diarrhea, unexplained weight loss, unexplained weight gain, mood swings, diarrhea—*"

Mom rolls her eyes. "Yeah, but—"

"*—Dizziness, trouble sleeping, trouble with authority, forgotten passwords, memories of past lives—*"

I jump in: "*Visions of* future *lives, a fear of clouds—*"

"*—Songs stuck in your head, the urge to adopt a goat—*

"*The urge to* be *a goat—*"

"*Constipation—*"

"OK, OK!" Mom says. "You're getting the TMS, though. That's the important thing."

"Of course she's getting it," I say. "Who *wouldn't* want the chance to remember their past life as Cleopatra?"

The doctor walks in, pulling the TMS machine behind her.

Mom motions for Grandma to put her phone away. She doesn't.

"Will this help with her memory problems?" Mom asks the doctor.

Without looking up from her phone, Grandma says, "I don't have memory problems." *Blimey!* "Doctor, do you mean to tell me you've never gotten anybody's name wrong? Come on now." *Well, blow me down!*

The doctor answers cautiously: "I *have*, yes … But the type of dementia you have is known to affect memory. And the disease progresses over time. So, it's important that we—"

"I don't know why y'all keep saying I have dementia. I'm fine."

"Let's just give the treatment a try, shall we?" She does jazz hands, rattling the bangle bracelets under the sleeves of her white coat.

"Think of it as a spa day for your brain. What do you say?"

Grandma ignores her. *Fire in the hole!*

While the doctor sets up the TMS machine, Mom asks her how long this is going to last. And I can tell she doesn't just mean the TMS treatment.

"I'll be honest with you because if I were in your position, I'd want someone to be honest with me. This could all be over in a few months. Or a few years. Or many years. We just don't know. There's no way to predict."

I'm thrilled. I'd love to have my old grandma back in a few months—to talk to her without being called Bella; to put a puzzle together with her and not worry she'll get that Halloween-mask look if a piece is missing. Then I realize that's not the kind of "over" the doctor is talking about, and I feel a little carsick.

The doctor places the "hat" on Grandma's head.

*Blimey!*

Mom says, "You've got to quit playing that game now, OK? Put the phone away."

"Don't tell me what to do. No matter how old you get, just remember this: I'll always be your mother."

Mom says, "If you don't put the phone away, it can mess up the TMS, and you'll have to come back here and get zapped all over again." I'm pretty sure she made that part up, but it gets Grandma to put her phone back in her purse.

The doctor clasps the strap under Grandma's chin and tightens it. "Oh, you *do* get to come back tomorrow," she says in a pep-rally voice. "In fact, you'll come back four more days in a row. That's how long the TMS series takes."

Mom texts me while the doctor pushes some buttons on the machine: "Why would the doc tell her that? I was going to wait until the morning of. Now we'll have to hear your grandma gripe about it all day."

Grandma says, "Y'all crazy. I'm not coming here for five days because I called Louisa her mom's name one time. Anybody could make a mistake like that. And they look so much alike. And she was just *standing* there, with her mom's favorite ice cream on a tray next to her."

Mom gasps. She turns to me. "*You've* been eating my Crick-or-Treat?"

Grandma laughs. "Like *I* would eat bugs?"

I think fast: "Hey, Grandma. You'll never believe what I saw online the other day: a video of you in the rodeo. 1998. Here, I'll send it to you. You can watch it on your phone when the TMS is over. I'll send it to you, too, Mom."

"What event was it?" Grandma asks. "Calf roping?"

"Barrel racing."

"Ah! My best one!"

"Stay still for me," the doctor says. Then she notices Grandma's foot in her sparkly flip-flop: "Oh! Your foot's looking a little rough there. You should probably make an appointment with your primary care physician—get that looked at."

"I took first place in barrel racing, you know." The trophy says third place, but I don't correct her. "Yeah, me and Angel took first place that time. And I had a sprained ankle that day. I remember. Racing on a sprained ankle! Can you imagine? I tell you what: if Angel were here right now, we'd still be able to finish a barrel race in 15 seconds. Angel had complete trust in me. I mean, she didn't trust anybody else, but she sure did trust *me*. She'd rest her head on my shoulder."

Grandma tries to lean her head to the side, as if Angel were on her shoulder right now and nuzzling her, but the doctor says, "Head straight, please."

"And when I rode her, it was like all my problems melted away. The whole world could have been going to hell in a handbasket, and I wouldn't have cared. Because it's peaceful in the saddle."

The doctor dims the lights.

"Some might say Angel was just a dumb animal, but she was my friend. My real friend. I never felt lonely when I was with her. She understood me. We understood each other."

I think of Callisto. I remember telling Callisto that Ezra and I shared a blanket at the beach. I remember telling her that Mom was being unfair for turning off my data just because I wouldn't clean my room. I remember telling her that it wasn't *Mom's* room, and nobody was forcing her to come in here, so why should *she* care if it was clean or not?

"I understand you, too," I say.

# CHAPTER 15

In the pet store, while Grandma looks at the eels, Mom and I go to quote-unquote "check out the aquarium filters," but really we just whisper to each other.

"Grandma's *peeing* herself?"

"I should have mentioned it to the doctor just now," Mom says. She clenches her hands into fists. "I'm so mad at myself. Why didn't I say anything? I guess I figured your grandma would just deny it? And I didn't want to embarrass anybody. But still, I should have said *something*." She shakes her head again. "Why didn't I do it? I was right there."

"Did she *tell* you she's peeing herself?"

"Of course not. She didn't want me to know. Probably thinks I still don't know. She's been hiding her ... you know, *wet* clothes in the laundry. But once I realized what was happening, it was pretty obvious. I didn't bring it up, though. Just washed her clothes and hung them out to dry and actually folded them and put them away for once. I mean, I didn't want to make her feel bad. You understand."

"Yeah, for sure. I understand totally." Except I don't understand—not completely, anyway. Like, if I were to keep peeing *my* pants and Mom found out about it, she would get onto me for hiding it, rush me to the doctor—all freaked out about it—or both. But maybe it's different when you're dealing with your own mother who's doing the hiding and the peeing.

Mom tells me how Grandma's dementia is a progressive disease and how it's only going to get worse from here on out—how it *is* getting worse—even though the doctor just said all of that less than an hour ago, and Mom herself already told me all of this months ago, and Glazier has been telling me all of this every time I say, "OK, Glazier: Does dementia run in families?" (not usually) and, "OK, Glazier: Is it true that eating really spicy foods keeps you from getting dementia?" (no, that's just a myth).

She tells me about the CT scans Grandma has had. She tells me Grandma's brain looks like Swiss cheese. She tells me about the all-day psychological test she took a year ago: "Do you know what month it is?" "Who is the president?" "What were the three words I asked you to remember when you started this test?"

Mom says, "I didn't tell you all these gory details. I didn't want to weigh you down with all that. I mean, bruh, you're just a kid. A mature kid, but still. It's like when *I* was growing up, and I'd hear about how the world was getting hotter and the honeybees were dying and blah blah blah, and there wasn't anything I could do about any of it. But I guess ..." She sighs. "Look, I'm just tired, OK? I'm tired. It wears you out, keeping a secret. And if I don't talk to *someone* about this, I'll explode. Unfortunately, that someone is you."

Finally we go back to Grandma. She's carrying a shopping basket with a bag of fish in it. No. She's got *bags* of fish. Bags of mollies and guppies and eels and neon tetras and cory catfish and—what is this thing?—one yellow snail.

At least she didn't get goldfish.

"Grandma, these won't fit in your tank. You have way too many fish. *Way* too many."

She smiles. "I know."

"You ... you *know*?"

"Yeah! The girl who works here is getting me a bigger tank right now."

Mom and I stare at her.

"She'll have it up front for me when I check out."

We stare some more.

"It's a 40-gallon."

Somewhere in the store, the squeak of a dog toy breaks whatever spell we're under. Mom's like, "Where are you going to put a 40-gallon fish tank? It's sure as heck not going to fit where your little tank is now."

"I know."

Now it's Mom's turn to say, "*You know?*"

Grandma smiles again. I'm starting to think she planned this all out. "That fish girl got me an aquarium stand. It'll be up there when we check out, too. Mahogany. Real nice. You'll like it."

Grandma hands Mom the shopping basket. Mom's so shocked that she takes it without saying anything. She just glares at the basket and squeezes the handle so hard that her knuckles turn white.

Grandma heads toward the cash register. She looks back at us. "Y'all coming?"

# CHAPTER 16

Today I get mail from Ezra. Not a text. Not a photo. A piece of actual mail, in the actual mailbox.

Grandma watches me open the envelope, but she's supposed to be paying attention to the doctor's appointment she's in the middle of. Mom is holding up Grandma's phone and saying, "Tell the doctor how long your foot has been hurting," but Grandma's looking at me, craning her neck to try to see the return address on the envelope.

"Who's it from?" she asks me.

"If you finally broke down and got yourself a pair of smart glasses, you'd be able to zoom in and find out."

Mom taps Grandma on the knee. "The doctor is *talking* to you."

I take the envelope to my room and close the door. Inside is a sheet of heavy, capital-A *Artiste* paper, folded into perfect thirds. This must be the 400-series canvas paper Ezra was talking about.

For a few seconds, I don't unfold it. I don't want to see the break-up letter that I know is written on it. *This is hard to say, but Lydia and I just have so much in common ...*

Only it isn't a break-up letter. It isn't a letter at all. It's a drawing. Of Mera. Except it's drawn entirely in gold and silver paint. And she's wearing glasses. And she's wearing a charm bracelet.

It's *me*. It's a drawing of *me* as Mera.

In the bottom right-hand corner of the page, he's written in pencil, "L—I drew this using only the 101st and 102nd paint pens. You were right. They're the only metallic ones. But they don't shine as bright as you. Love, E—"

# CHAPTER 17

*"But they don't shine as bright as yoooou."*

"What? What's wrong with it?"

Grandma rolls her eyes but doesn't answer.

"What?" I smack her gently on her daisy tattoo. "*What?*"

"I don't trust this kid, is all I'm saying. Now, calm down, calm down: I don't mean he's cheating on you or anything like that. I just mean he's insincere, and he doesn't even know it. He reminds me of your grandfather. There's a reason you never met him and your mom *barely* met him. If you'd have asked him, he'd have told you that he was the sweetest guy in the world—always buying me little gifts and saying how pretty I was—but I don't think he ever really listened to a word I said. Oh, he loved to tell *me* about *his* work and *his* hobbies. Like, the time he got a drone? My God. He wouldn't shut *up* about that thing. And whenever he played video games, he'd want me to watch him play because he said, that way, we were doing it together. And if I was in another room, he'd be like, 'Babe! Hey, babe! You've got to see this! Babe!' and then I'd go in there, and he'd do a slow-mo replay of how he took out some bad guy using his character's special move.

"And, the thing is, I *liked* watching him play video games. That was fine. But did he ever watch *me* play video games? No. Did he ever come out and watch me and Angel in the rodeo? No. But, boy, he'd *say* he cared about me and Angel and the rodeo, wouldn't he? And I think he even believed that he did. That's what I mean about his being insincere without knowing it."

"OK, but the thing is, Grandma, that was a whole other person. *I'm* talking about Ezra. It's a totally different situation."

"Uh-huh."

"Ezra's not insincere. Not at all. He's too nice to be insincere."

"Oh, please. Nice people can be the least sincere ones out there. But tell me why you like him then. Go on. If he's such a great, *nice* guy, it should be easy."

"He's a really good artist. You should see his drawings. He's making a graphic novel called *The Shaman.* It's about a shaman. Obviously. Actually, it's not just a graphic novel. It's going to be this whole series, and—"

"Yeah, but why do you *like* him?"

Mom's bedroom door flies open. She's wearing one of her "work" blazers—the hemp one with the blue, plastic buttons that shimmer like peacock feathers—and a white blouse that I know she didn't bother to iron anywhere the blazer covers it. She's also wearing cut-off jean shorts; they won't show up on camera. She stares at us.

"Is your meeting over?" I ask.

"Yes. Why are you two lying on the kitchen floor?"

"It's cooler down here," I say. "You should try it."

"You should," Grandma says. "Just lift the back of your shirt up and put your bare back against the linoleum. I don't know why I didn't try it before."

"You look ridiculous," Mom says, slipping off her blazer. I was right: her sleeves are rumpled. The armpits of her blouse are see-through with sweat. She hangs her blazer on the back of a kitchen chair. "And anyway, Mom, now that you're down there, how do you plan on getting back up?"

"Oh, I'll do it."

"Right."

"I *will*."

Mom unhooks her bra and holds up the back of her blouse. She sits down on the floor next to Grandma. "Ridiculous." She lies back. She sighs and closes her eyes. "Absolutely ridiculous."

We lie there for 30 seconds or 10 minutes—I can't tell—without talking or laughing or anything. In the living room, somebody is killing an alien with a flamethrower, and the alien is shrieking, and then it's just grilled-burger noises. Outside, a dog is barking, and somebody is blasting grassmetal as they drive by: banjos and fiddles and drums and screaming. But here in the kitchen, the three of us don't make a sound. I try to imagine constellations in the bumps and cracks on the ceiling. There. Those cracks look like a windowpane. And over there. Those bumps are a firework. I try to find a pattern that looks like Leo—my Zodiac sign—but I don't find anything. But hey! There's Mickey Mouse!

Then Mom goes and ruins the quiet: "Your foot's looking worse, Mom."

I nudge her. "Oh, hush. You're always bothering Grandma about her foot. It's like how you're always bothering me about my tics. Just let people be."

Grandma says, "Uh-huh, that's right!"

Mom props herself up on her elbows. "Now, look. Listen." Here it comes. "You've got to see your doctor about that foot, Mom. I'm serious. If it's infected, and if the infection gets bad enough, you could die."

Grandma laughs.

Mom slaps the linoleum. "I'm *serious*. Just look at her foot, Louisa. I mean it. Look at it."

So I look. The spot on the bottom of her foot is bigger now. It's redder, too—the color of

Mom's red velvet cake. It's a good thing I already kind of hate red velvet cake because seeing this would have ruined it for me.

Grandma pats my hand. "Tell her it doesn't look that bad."

I stand up. "I should get ready for hapkido."

Grandma wraps her hand around my ankle. "Just tell her, Louisa." I try to step away, but she won't let go. "Tell her there's nothing wrong with me. Tell her I'm fine."

I do kick one—the shin kick—just to break free of her grip. "Really, I'm going to be late. Aren't I, Mom? I've got to go."

# CHAPTER 18

Ruby unbuckles her sandal, takes it off, and slides it under her chair. "So." She does the same thing with her other sandal. "Samhain."

"So." I step out of my flip-flops and put them under my chair, too. "Samhain." We're sitting side by side in the entry room, next to the crane fountain. "You know, I feel kind of weird asking what it is—"

"No, no! Don't feel weird!"

"—and, like, maybe I should already know what it is?"

"No! Don't feel weird at all! It's—"

"Or maybe I should just look it up myself? Like, 'Sure, let me ask my glasses about that for you, even though you have your own glasses, on your own face, right now.'"

"Well, it's not exactly as widely known as Halloween is. Samhain is the holiday my parents celebrate on October 31. Because they're, you know"—she whispers this next part—"Wiccan."

I whisper back: "Wiccan? Like, witches?"

She glances around the room to make sure no one is standing too close to her. She looks like she's trying to shoplift lip gloss. "Remember that picture I showed you of my grandma, and how you said she looked like a witch?"

"Yeah."

"Well, she looked like a witch because she *was* a witch."

"Your grandma was a *witch*?"

"But not a Wicked Witch of the West witch? Know what I mean?"

I nod, but I don't.

"She's Wiccan, and she raised my mom Wiccan. Or, really it's more like Wiccan-adjacent. My mom likes to joke and call it 'Wiccan't.' When my mom and my dad got together in college, my *other* grandma—my *abuela*—hated it." My glasses whisper *grandmother* in my left ear. "She thought my mom was evil. According to my dad, she'd go around like, 'How could my sweet, little angel baby fall in love with that *bruja*?'" *Witch*, my glasses whisper. "But he married my mom anyway, and the rest is history."

As I turn the translator off, I say, "So, your grandma's a witch."

"Yes."

"And your mom's a witch."

"Yes."

"And *you're* a witch."

"*What?* No! I'm a geologist. At least, I *want* to be. One day."

"They don't wear a pointy hat, right? Or, like, a robe?"

"I mean, my grandma grubs around the house in a bathrobe. Does that count?" She laughs. "It's not really a big deal—their being Wiccan, I mean. I swear, they only have their Samhain parties because it's an excuse to drink expensive wine in the yard and lie on the trampoline. And before you ask: no, they don't do curses or hexes or anything like that. They only do good spells because they believe that whatever energy they put out there will come back to them threefold." She adjusts her crooked hapkido belt until the knot is perfectly centered. "They do a lot of shadow work, too. Like, *so* much shadow work. They're always going on and on about it."

"Shadow work is *good*? Because it sounds, you know ..." I do jump-scare monster hands at her.

"Yeah, it's good, it's good. It's pretty much ... it's a form of meditation, almost. It's totally something my therapist would have me do. Like, she'd be all"—Ruby crosses her legs, folds her hands over her knee, and cocks her head to one side—"'*Maybe if you imagine taking this chemistry test and sit in attentive silence with the anxiety that arises, you'll befriend the anxiety and be calmer when you actually sit down to take the test.*'"

"Hey, me too! I mean, I go to therapy, too!" What am I doing? Why am I announcing this? "You know, for my tics. Which I, you know, have. Sometimes." Shut up, shut up, shut up.

Master Avery saves me by scaring the bejesus out of me. She grabs my shoulders and goes, "Boo!"

I jump.

Ruby tells me she does that all the time, to everybody, and that eventually you get used to it. Master Avery says it's true and that by the time I'm an orange belt, it won't scare me anymore. I'll have nerves of steel. And, by the way, she wanted to talk to me for a second. Am I enjoying the class?

I tell her I am. Because what else am I supposed to say? But also? I kind of *don't* hate it, actually?

"Excellent. And do you think you're going to stick with it after the trial period ends? Because we're almost at that point. And *you're* almost ready to test for your first stripe."

I'm not sure what testing for a stripe means. "Really?"

"Yes, really. You and a lot of other people are on my list. I've got some catching up to do. Do you think you could stick around for a few minutes after class ends? We can do yours today. Now, wait, hold on: don't panic, *mija*. I can tell you're freaking out. You're ready. I'm confident you'll do well. If I weren't confident, I wouldn't be testing you."

I look at Ruby, like *help!*

"It's just the stuff we've been working on, Louisa," she says. "You've done these things in class with me. You know: the thumb lock? the spearhead pressure point?"

I can barely remember these moves right now, even though I know Ruby is right: I've done them in class a million times. It's like when you're trying to spell your name for somebody over the phone, and next thing you know, a Category 5 mental hurricane has blown half of the English language out of your brain: "*L* as in *llama. O* as in *octopus. U* as in ... *underwear. A* as in ... *eyeball.* No, wait. That's an *E.*"

"I believe in you," Ruby says. "I'll stick around to cheer you on and everything. I mean, you're, like, my friend, right?"

*I'm, like, her friend, right?*

I try to look her in the eye, but I can't, so I look her in the earring. "OK, yeah," I tell the silver stud in her right ear, "I can stay late today. I'll do it."

"Excellent," Master Avery says again. "Really, don't worry: I'm only testing you on a few techniques. This stripe test is more like a progress report that comes before your report card. Your *belt* test is the report card, and that won't be for a few weeks." I'm nodding as she's talking, but I'm not really listening. Something about there being a stripe test *and* a belt test? I'm too busy staring at Ruby's earlobe and wondering if she has a second piercing, or if she *had* a second piercing and let it grow shut. Master Avery goes on: "And, it sounds to me like you're planning on being a permanent student. Is that right?"

Ruby starts a chant that's quieter than a hanger sliding across a closet rod. But then the chant gets louder. "Do. It. *Do. It. Do! It!*" She stomps her bare feet with each word. "*Do! It! Do! It!*"

"OK, fine, I'll do it, I'll do it." I look at Master Avery. "I mean, I was fixing to tell you," I lie.

Ruby's like, "You're going to love it. You really are. You're going to get your yellow belt and learn all these whole *other* basic kicks, and then you're going to get your orange belt and learn all these wrist escapes, and then you're going to get your green belt and learn your spin kick, and then—"

"Hold on there, *mija*. Let's not get ahead of ourselves. We don't want to overwhelm Louisa here." Master Avery looks at me. "You're not overwhelmed, are you?"

"No." Yes.

"All right." But I can tell she doesn't believe me. She goes behind the front desk and gets out her basket of yarn and crochet hooks. She takes out a miniature, crocheted yellow belt attached to a keyring, and she bows as she hands it to me. I bow as I take it. It's as soft as the lint I clean out of the lint trap when Mom gets onto me about how I have to help maintain the dryer and how the last thing we need is another housefire.

"Your next goal," Master Avery says. "Now, you girls had better get a move on. Class is going to start in"—she looks at the clock in the corner of her right lens—"about five minutes."

Once we're all lined up in the big mat room and ready to practice, Master Avery opens the supply closet where she keeps the kick pads and rolls out a big, blue ball—the kind you do sit-ups on. I don't know why, but I feel like whatever this is, it's going to be bad. Tons of sit-ups, maybe. Or worse: dodgeball.

"Now, for those of you who've never seen these ... Wait. Raise your hand if you've never used one of these in here."

I'm one of the few people in the room to raise their hand. Everyone looks at me, or at least it feels like they are. My stomach feels like spaghetti sloshing around in a colander.

Master Avery must be able to tell I'm nervous-slash-embarrassed because she says that's OK; she doesn't expect any of us to know what these are the first time we see them. "They're called *u-ke-mi* balls: u-k-e-m-i. Ruby, do you remember what *ukemi* is Japanese for?"

"Falling, ma'am."

Uh-uh. No way.

"That's right. Falling. We use these balls to practice our falls. Today what I'd like us to work on is our forward break-falls. And when you start out—you white and yellow belts—it's really simple. Really gentle. You just kneel in front of the ball, like this"—she demonstrates—"turn your head to the side, and press your knee against the ball. Then just hug the ball tight and give a *biiig* push with your legs. Not a big push. Not a *big* push. A *biiig* push. What kind of push?"

We all answer together: "A *biiig* push."

"You'll roll over the ball and be completely safe. Really"—she looks at me—"you'll be absolutely, positively safe. Just hug the ball. Just *be* the ball." She rolls herself over the ball and lands on her side, with a *bang*.

"Now, after you've gotten good at falling *with* the ball, you can learn how to fall without it. It's the same thing, really. You kneel; you keep your head down; you push yourself over; you roll over your shoulder." She sets the ball aside and demonstrates this, too. "Eventually you can leap into the fall. Like this. Ruby, come here." She smiles and points at the ground. "Be a shrub."

Ruby goes to the middle of the mat and curls up like a turtle hiding in its shell. Somebody giggles. The whole room is full of waiting, like a movie theater when the trailers end and the lights go down and you're like *wait, did I silence my glasses?*

"Now, let's pretend you're running from a junkyard dog." Who the heck breaks into a junkyard? Do junkyards even *have* dogs? "And then you get to a little shrub that you have to jump over." She trots toward Ruby. And just when I think she's going to trip over her, Master Avery turns into, like, Supergirl. Her feet leave the ground. She's airborne; she's flying. And then she's somersaulting on the mat. And then she's standing back up again and jogging to the other end of the mat like it's nothing—like she's not a 62-year-old on calcium supplements.

"Thank you, Ruby. You were an excellent shrub."

Ruby laughs and goes back to her place in line. She doesn't look like she was scared at all. She's been a shrub before. Lots of times.

Master Avery puts the ball on the left half of the mat and makes me and the three yellow belts line up behind it. I'm last. Thank God. The orange and green belts line up in the middle of the mat, behind nothing. The blue and brown belts line up on the right half of the mat, also behind nothing.

I should probably be watching the yellow belts to see how they practice this fall, but instead I'm watching Ruby as she runs at full speed, launches herself through the air, rolls across the mat, springs back up, does a high heel front kick at her reflection, and casually goes to the back of the line like she *didn't* just do a real-life Mera-fighting-Black Manta move, like she's just lining up to get off a bus or order some cheese wontons.

Then I watch Charlotte slowly stand up from her chair, do the same somersault everyone else is doing, and walk back to her chair with the heavy, careful steps of someone wearing steel-toed boots that are three sizes too big. She sits in her chair and wheels to the back of the line so the next person can go, and no one but me seems to find it amazing that a girl in a wheelchair just did this thing. She's done it before. Everyone is used to it. Just like they're used to people being shrubs. Just like my mom is used to my tics. Move along, people; nothing to see here, nothing to see.

"Hey," the yellow belt behind me says, "it's your turn."

I just stare at the ball. Master Avery comes around and tells me—again—what I'm supposed to be doing, but I'm still frozen. So she poses me on top of the ball, like a Barbie, grabs the back of my belt, and says, "What kind of push should you do?"

"A big push. I mean, a big push, ma'am."

"No. A *biiig* push." And even though I don't do any kind of push—big or *biiig* or small or *smaaall*—Master Avery pulls on my belt, and my feet are over my head, and then they're not, and I'm lying on the mat, and the ball is bouncing away.

"See? You did it." No, I didn't. *She* did it. "Just hold on a little tighter next time."

# CHAPTER 19

"Don't hold it so tight," Mom says. "I'm trying to get it even."

I loosen my grip on the sparkly garland of leaves. Mom tugs on her end of it. It threads through my hands, and orange glitter goes everywhere.

"There now," she says, looping a spirally vine around the last hook in the doorframe. "Is it even?"

I can't tell. I'm too close. I'd ask Grandma, but she's asleep with her feet propped up. She's taking medicine for her foot now, but it doesn't look better—at least not to *me*, it doesn't—and now there's a big, yellowish blister on it.

I get down from the chair I've been standing on, take a few steps back, and consider the whole front door. "It's perfect."

Mom fluffs some of the gold and orange leaves and gets down from her chair to check out the garland herself.

"Why do you do that?" I say. "Why do you ask what I think and then you look at it anyway?"

She squints at it. "I think it's too long on the left."

"Oh my God."

"And it's saggy in the middle."

"Oh my *God*."

"Come on, come on, come on." We get back on our chairs. Mom tugs at the garland, and one of the hooks peels off the doorframe. She presses it back into place, but then she drops her end of the garland. Now the doorframe looks like somebody waxed off half their eyebrow.

Mom covers her face with her hands. Her shoulders shake.

"Are you crying or laughing?"

"Yes."

"Mom, it's just a garland, relax."

She wipes her eyes. "I wish I had a dollar for every time somebody has told me to relax. We'd all be living in a mansion right now—

*relaxing.*" She picks up the garland. As she hangs it back up, she glances over her shoulder to make sure Grandma's still asleep. "Hey," she says quietly. "I've been looking into The Harbor for your Grandma. You know, the assisted-living facility. The one by hapkido."

"The mosh place?"

She nods. "That fire has me scared. Really scared. And the incontinence is ..." She rubs the back of her arm. "I mean, in a way, I'm glad we moved here when we did because if we hadn't, who knows what would have happened to her if she were still living alone? She could have burned the house down. She could have wrecked her car again and gotten hurt, or hurt somebody else, or—"

"It wasn't a wreck," Grandma interrupts, startling me. "It was a fender bender."

"You're up!" Mom says, sounding too happy. "You had a good nap there, didn't you?"

Grandma gives her side-eye. "What are y'all talking about?"

Mom and I look at each other.

"We were just talking about how nice The Harbor at Mill Creek Plaza looked," Mom says. "I wish *I* could live in a place like that. A life of leisure. Nothing to worry about." She sounds like she's trying to convince a little kid to eat their "fairy trees" which are actually boiled broccoli.

"I'm not moving to The Harbor," Grandma says.

"Oh, I'm not saying you *have* to move there." Mom busies herself with arranging the vines around the garland in spiraling swoops. "*I'm* just saying you might like living at a place like that—you know, *one* day. I mean, think about it: you'd never have to cook your own lunch again because there's a food court right there."

"But I like to cook."

"And they have a different activity planned for almost every day. There's an activity director and everything. Doesn't that sound fun?"

"I don't need an activity director. I have plenty of activities as it is. I play games—"

"You watch other people play games," Mom interrupts.

"And I play games myself, too." She gestures to her Switch, which I know for a fact she hasn't charged in the whole time I've been here. "I do puzzles. I cook."

"Your cooking set the kitchen on fire."

"I take care of my fish."

"Louisa takes care of your fish."

"Oh, I do lots of things. Lots. Now, can one of y'all get me the marshmallows? Louisa, hon, go get me the marshmallows. Please and thank you."

I make sure my end of the garland is good and secure on the hooks because I'm pretty sure if it falls again, Mom's going to have a breakdown. In the kitchen, I open a cabinet and move stuff out of the way—a sticky container of peaches, a can of probably-expired beans, four almost-empty bags of rice—until I see the marshmallows in the back. All three bags are already open.

"Do you want the coconut-covered ones, the chocolate-covered ones, or the ones shaped like bats?"

Grandma laughs. "Like I said, bring me the marshmallows."

I try one of the coconut ones. It's stale.

I bring all three bags into the living room. Mom takes one look at me and says, "Whoa, whoa, whoa. Three bags of marshmallows is way too much."

"Well, good Lord, Bella, don't be ridiculous. I don't plan on eating all of them."

"And I didn't plan on moving back in with my mother when I was 40 freaking years old, but here I am." She takes a deep breath and makes *ommm* hands. "OK," she says. "OK. Why don't we at least check your sugar first."

"*We* aren't doing anything."

"I'll just take a quick—"

"Louisa, give me the marshmallows, hon."

I don't know who I should listen to—Mom or Grandma—but Grandma's older, so I guess that means she's sort of the highest belt rank here, even if she has dementia. So, I hand her the marshmallows. She sets the chocolate ones and the bat ones next to her new, huge fish tank—between a porcelain baby shoe and an empty Kleenex box—and puts the coconut ones in her lap. She takes one out of the bag. "Louisa, girl, how'd you get glitter on these?" She squints at it. "No, wait. It's just coconut." She pops it in her mouth. She grimaces. "Nope. Glitter."

Mom gets down from her chair. "I'm just going to take a look at—Mom, don't spit it out in the Kleenex box. Like, really? *Really?*" She's pushing up Grandma's sleeve when an invitation from Ruby pops up on my glasses: Samhain party, 6:00–???, October 31.

"Hey, Mom, there's this ... Samhain party, which is like a Halloween party, only not."

She looks up from Grandma's tattoo. Her smile is as bright as a halved orange. "Yes, you can go."

"But you haven't heard me say anything about it yet. Like, literally nothing."

"Is it a friend of yours?"

"Yes."

"Do you trust them?"

"Yes!"

"Then you can go. Have fun. Take the car. Be home by midnight."

I laugh. "Mom, have you lost it? I can't take the car. I don't have a license yet."

"It drives itself."

Grandma shakes her head. "I still don't like that thing."

I'm like, "It's illegal. And why are you in such a hurry to agree to this party?"

And Mom's like, "Because I want you to make friends. Your sugar's fine, Mom, but go easy on the marshmallows." She puts Grandma's sleeve back down.

Grandma stuffs three coconut-covered marshmallows in her mouth at the same time. She mumbles around the half-chewed marshmallows: "Oh, God. You didn't fall in with the Druids, did you?"

I'm like, "What are you talking about—Druids? She's Wiccan. Or, at least, her parents are Wiccans. She's ... I don't know what *she* is. Probably nothing, I don't know."

"Because the Druids are a pyramid scheme."

"They ... what?"

"Yup. True story. I gave one of those Druids 50 bucks for a box of magic sticks. He said I'd be an independent retailer. But what am I going to do with 44 unsold dowsing rods now?"

"Mom, did you take your meds today?"

Grandma shakes her head. "Sneaky Druid jerks."

"*Mom.* Did you take your meds? Because I think you're confused."

"Yeah, I took them, Bella."

Mom squints at her. "Uh-huh."

"I *did.*"

Mom rolls her eyes. She turns to me and says she can only imagine how hard this move to Palma Linda has been on me—hitting reset on my whole life, starting at a new school, leaving all my friends behind.

"*And* my boyfriend," I say.

Grandma gasps. "Y'all." She leans close to her fish tank. She taps the glass. "*Y'all!*" She taps the glass again. "My frog is dead."

We stare at her.

"It's gone belly-up," she says. "Really."

I walk over to the tank. And there it is: a frog floating upside down on the surface of the water, above the shrimp that are darting through the hornwort and the Amazon sword plants that are turning yellow, and—hold on, why are the Amazon swords turning yellow? And, wait: is that a brown spot on one of the leaves?

"I'm sure it's just sleeping, Grandma." Except I'm not sure at all. I don't even remember where I heard that African dwarf frogs sleep on their backs. Or if I did.

Is that more algae on the skull? I thought I got rid of all the algae. And shouldn't the shrimp be eating the algae anyway?

I lift the aquarium lid.

"It'll wake up any second now."

I poke the frog. Now orange glitter is floating on the water next to it.

The frog doesn't move.

"Yup. Any second now."

# CHAPTER 20

"Don't move."

Ruby pulls down the lower lid of my right eye and starts to color my waterline turquoise, but halfway through, she pulls the eyeliner away. "I said don't move."

"I'm not moving."

"I don't want to poke you in the eye, because let me tell you, I've poked myself in the eye before when I was doing this, and it does *not* feel good. Not good at all."

"That doesn't inspire confidence."

She pulls my lid down again. The eyeliner burns, but I pretend not to mind.

"My Grandma's paranoid that you're all a bunch of Druids," I say.

"Don't make me laugh! I want to get the line straight!"

"She started talking about buying ... I don't know, dowsing rods from some Druids or whatever, but she probably just went to a yard sale and bought a Jenga set from a guy in a hoodie. Like, who even knows what's true anymore?"

"*Voila!*" She steps back from me.

I put on my glasses and look at myself in the practice room's wall of mirrors. I fine-tune how my long red wig frames my face, straighten my gold-seashell crown, and adjust my bracelet. "Perfect," I say.

"Not quite." Ruby rummages around in the makeup kit she brought with her, takes out a tube of lip gloss, unscrews the cap, and tells me to open my mouth. "No, not that much. Good. Just like that." She runs a wet wand of clear gloss over my bottom lip. Then she dips the wand in the tube and does the top lip, too. "There," she says, screwing the cap back on. "*Now* you're the perfect Mera."

"And you're the perfect ... what kind of geologist are you again?"

Ruby poses: hitches her thumbs on her toolbelt, holds her head up high, smiles like *cheeeese.* "A planetary geologist."

"*That's* right. And you're mining Mars for oxygen and nutrients."

Ruby pats me on the head. "You were paying attention. A-plus!"

I smooth down the corner of the American-flag patch pinned to her sleeve.

Charlotte sticks her head in the doorway. She's using a cane today—instead of the wheelchair—and she taps the doorframe with it to get our attention. "*Pssst*," she says, but if she's trying to be sneaky, she's failing, because she's wearing a Las Vegas showgirl costume, complete with a pink, feathered headdress. She's wound pink and white rope lights around her cane. "Hey, y'all," she whispers. "Class."

We barely make it to the mat in time to line up. Our class looks like a fever dream: a showgirl; a cowboy; two Elsas from *Frozen 4*; a zombie; a vampire; a cow; a yellow crayon; Lord Slothington, complete with top hat, monocle, and sloth-clawed gloves; Mera; and a space geologist. And we're being taught by a garden gnome.

The garden gnome tells us we'll all be working on a blue-belt technique today. For green belts and down—that's me—it'll be a look ahead at what's to come. For blue belts and up—that's Ruby—it'll be a review.

"Can anyone tell me one of the three most important parts of punch defense?" Master Avery holds up three fingers. Her nails are painted green to match her pointy cap.

Oscar says, "Movement," at the same moment that Charlotte, Ruby, and Em—the pregnant woman, who's one of the Elsas—raise their hands.

Master Avery nods toward Charlotte. "Thank you for raising your hand, Charlotte. What's one of the most important parts of punch defense?"

"Movement."

Master Avery puts down one finger. Now she's making a peace sign. "Good. Movement. Anyone else?"

This time Oscar waits to be called on. "Eye contact."

Master Avery puts down one more finger. Now she looks like she's signaling to get a waiter's attention. "Yes. Eye contact. Who remembers the third thing? Ruby?"

"Timing."

No more fingers. "That's right. Movement, eye contact, and timing. Now, Oscar, would you come and sucker-punch me please? *That's* a sentence you would only ever hear in the *dojang*."

We all watch as a cow punches the garden gnome. The gnome lifts her arm to block the punch. Then the gnome looks at us and asks if it was a good punch defense or not.

No, Em says. The defense wasn't good. Why? Because Master Avery didn't step away from the punch. She didn't move her feet at all.

"That right, Em. Now, I know what you're all thinking: 'Duh, Master Avery. It's obvious you have to move.' But here in a minute, I'm going to partner you up, and just watch: some of you will forget to move at least once. It happens."

She has Oscar punch her again, but this time, she exaggerates a big, diagonal step, and the bell jingles on her red, curly-toed shoe. She demonstrates the correct way to do it, over and over again. "Step and block. Step and block. *Entonces.*"

My glasses whisper, "So," in my right ear. I don't even bother turning off the translator this time because what's the point? And besides: I don't want to fool with it while Master Avery is telling Charlotte that she's partners with me, and Charlotte and I are headed onto the mat together, and I'm punching at her feathery, Dr. Seuss-character-looking head.

But Charlotte doesn't just use her arm to block my punches. Sometimes she uses her cane. She swoops it in a big circle—like an actress in an old-timey musical—and taps me on a spot just above my wrist that makes my whole arm feel like there's an electrical current running through it. And the whole time, I'm thinking, how does she aim so well—with her arm and especially with the cane? Like, how does she manage to hit me in just the right spot every single time? So I ask her. Because most of the time, I end up hitting the bad guy closer to their elbow, which barely hurts at all. And she says it just comes with time, and all I have to do is keep practicing because—trust her—she was the same way when she was a white belt.

"Normally people don't learn these cane techniques until they're a second-degree black belt," Charlotte says as she taps me with the cane again. "But Master Avery made an exception for me because of my HSP. That's the disorder I have. It makes walking hard because my legs get stiff and weak. If I'm just moving around my house"—*tap*—"I can usually get by without the cane because there's enough furniture around to lean on if I need to." *Tap*. "But if I'm going to, like, the dentist, I'll usually bring my cane, and if I'm going to the grocery store, I'll break out the chair." *Tap*. "I like to practice hapkido with the chair, with the cane, and with nothing because—"

"I'm hearing a lot of chitchat, everyone," Master Avery says. "I know we're wearing costumes today, but we still need to be martial."

So, for a while, the only sounds I hear are *kiyups*, the swish of feet sliding over the mat, the jingling of Master Avery's hat, and the occasional clank of Oscar's cowbell. But then Glazier picks up someone talking in a foreign language and translates it for me, and what I hear makes me freeze in the middle of blocking one of Charlotte's punches: "Yes, Louisa is very nice."

Charlotte's like, "OK, you weren't even looking at me that time. You have to focus. You've got this."

But I'm like, "*Sssh!*" Because, seriously, did she not hear that? Does she have her translator turned off? Are her glasses *not* garbage?

I look around. Whoever was talking about me has to be close enough on the mat that my glasses would pick up on what they're saying. That person also has to know me well enough to say whether I am, in fact, nice.

Only one person fits that description: Ruby. She's chatting with Master Avery while her partner, Oscar, stares off into space and fidgets with his cowbell.

I tell Charlotte, "Sorry, just, give me a second. My glasses are acting up. I should turn them off." It's not *exactly* a lie. I pretend to fiddle with them, like I'm trying to turn them off, but really I'm just waiting to see if they translate more of the conversation. They don't, though. That's the only sentence in a foreign language—Spanish, I'm sure—that was loud and clear enough for them to understand. *Yes, Louisa is very nice.*

I spend the rest of class thinking about it. Does Ruby think I'm *nice*-nice, or does she think I'm *Grandpa*-nice? Was Master Avery asking Ruby if she likes being partnered up with me in class? Was she asking if Ruby likes me as a friend—or as *more than* a friend? But why should that even pop into my head? Why should I care if she likes me in *that* way? It's ridiculous. She knows I have a boyfriend. I'm sure I mentioned Ezra to her at some point. Didn't I?

I flip through our conversations, like scrolling through the animal-vision filters on my glasses. *No. Nope. Not that time. Not that time either.*

My God: it's possible she has no idea I'm in a quote-unquote "relationship."

I mean, *a relationship.*

There's nothing quote-unquote about it. Why did I think that?

By the end of class, Charlotte seems annoyed with me, and I can't really blame her, because I've mentally checked out. But I also can't care that I annoyed her, because I'm too busy rushing over to Ruby at the shoe rack—without making it *look* like I'm rushing to her—so I can blurt out, "Hey, do you want to come over for dinner, my mom's making chicken and dumplings right now, and she always makes a ton—enough to eat for dinner *and* supper and still have leftovers tomorrow—which means there's plenty for you, and we can rideshare, if you don't want to that's OK too, I understand, you're probably busy, I get it."

She picks up her sandals, lets them dangle from her fingers. The beaded tassels sway from the ankle straps. "Like, you mean, *now*?"

Oh, God. "Never mind, it's fine, it's last-minute, forget about it." I can't find my flip-flops. *What'd I do with my flip-flops?* "I mean you probably already had plans, and it's getting late"—what am I saying? It's barely noon on a Saturday—"and you know, like I said, you're probably busy, we can do it some other time or, you know, not."

Ruby picks up my flip-flops. They were on the bottom shelf, completely uncovered, in plain view. "Now is good."

While Ruby and I wait for our ride in the parking lot, I text Mom to let her know she's coming over. Mom says to give her more warning next time, but she doesn't end the text with a period, so I know she's not *really* mad about it.

When I text Grandma about it, she texts back, "Good! I like this girl a lot."

I start to say that I like this girl a lot, too, but I stop myself.

Grandma texts, "Are you on your way now?"

"Waiting for a ride in the parking lot."

"It's hotter than a crawfish boil on the surface of the sun. Go inside where it's cool."

"They can't bring the car INSIDE."

"Why are you still talking to me? Talk to HER."

"I'm talking to you because you're talking to me!"

# "SHUT UP AND TALK TO HER."

# CHAPTER 21

Nothing is on Grandma's coffee table. Nothing. Turns out, there's a compass rose painted on top of it, and I never knew.

The used tissues, crushed soda cans, stale chips, pistachio shells, and other things that used to be heaped next to Grandma's recliner are gone. Instead, there's just a shiny end table with nothing on it but a green, burning candle I've never seen before. And there's nothing surrounding the Halloween tree either. No dirty socks. No falling-down stacks of jigsaw puzzles. Just carpet with fresh vacuum tracks on it.

Grandma herself even looks neater, sitting there in her recliner with her feet up, wearing her llama slippers. At first I can't figure out *what* exactly looks so much neater about her, but then I realize it's her hair. Either she or Mom—probably Mom—parted it in the middle and curled it at the ends, so it looks like a gray bell.

Also: it smells like sixes in here. I take a closer look at the candle. The glass jar it's in has a picture of a meadow on it. It's called Summer Breeze.

Ruby takes off her space-geologist jacket. She's wearing a green tank top underneath, and there's a temporary rose tattoo on her arm. I realize I've never *seen* her arms before. It's like they're chiseled out of marble. I guess once you're a brown belt and you've thrown and pinned people enough times, you get to have Louvre arms like that.

She's still standing there, holding the jacket, and I'm like, "Oh! Here! Let me take that for you!" I hang it on the hall tree.

"Thank you for having me over, Mrs.—" Ruby looks at me. "OK, Louisa, this is so embarrassing, but I am totally blanking on your last name right now."

"Call me Bella. And this is my mom, Sarah."

But Grandma doesn't say anything. She just nods a little with a half-smile, like you do when someone tells you hi, but you can't remember who they are, and you have to fake it, and you're not totally sure they aren't saying hi to the person standing behind you anyway.

"It's nice to see you again, Bella. And Sarah. You know, I felt a little weird showing up in my costume, but Louisa told me you're really into Halloween"—she gestures to the Halloween tree—"so I guess it's not *so* weird?"

"Oh, please," Mom says. "You look fabulous. It's not weird at all. Where did you get all of the patches for your pants? Like, the Mars patch— is that from NASA?"

While Ruby explains how she ordered the patches online, I excuse myself to go to the bathroom, and I roll my eyes because *obviously she ordered the patches online.* What does Mom think she did? Drive to Cape Canaveral and mug an astronaut?

While I'm in the bathroom, I find myself willing Mom and Grandma not to talk about anything weird while I'm in here, like underboob sweat or K-pop. I'm also wishing Ruby won't bring up Samhain or bat skeletons.

When I open the cabinet to get more toilet paper, a Dr. Pepper can falls out. And there's more stuff hidden in there, too: napkins and tissues and food wrappers and laundry. I fling back the shower curtain: junk mail, jigsaw puzzles, a crusty fork, a plate with a plastic-looking glob of probably-barbecue-sauce on it. I look under the sink: the porcelain tree, the glass bell, the Switch. I can't decide if it was Mom or Grandma who did all this. Grandma would have been the one who wanted to impress Ruby, but Mom would have been the one to follow through on this idea. I like to think it was both of them. It makes me happy to think they worked on it together.

Most of the time, I'd just prop the new roll of toilet paper on top of the old one, which is just a cardboard tube now, but this time, I throw the old tube away and put the new roll on properly. I make sure all of the cabinets and the shower curtain are closed before I wash and dry my hands on a towel that is always, always damp, no matter how long we leave it on the towel rod. Then, before I leave, I straighten the towel and make sure it's perfectly centered on the rod. Even if it feels gross, at least it might *look* OK?

Back in the living room, I tell Ruby I was thinking of changing out of my costume, but I didn't want her to be the only person wearing one.

Mom perks up. "I can go put on my luna moth costume."

"No, Mom."

"Or my pirate costume. Or my—"

"*No.*"

Every topic at dinner is normal, thank God: "How is online school?" (good); "What do your parents do for a living?" (she's a pharmacist, he's an actuary, whatever that is); "You should go to the Veteran's Day parade, it's kind of a big deal here." (*OK, Glazier: When is Veteran's Day?*)

That's probably because Grandma doesn't talk at all. While Mom, Ruby, and I eat at the kitchen table, she eats in her recliner, with her plate balanced on the armrest. Only she doesn't exactly *eat.* She mainly pushes her food around in her bowl until she falls asleep, and the bowl tips, and probably-cold chicken and dumplings spill into her lap.

While Mom cleans her up, I get the idea to go practice hapkido in the field across the road.

I tell her it's *because I don't want Ruby to have to see all of that, OK? It's embarrassing.* Which may not be nice of me, but well, there it is. And, anyway, if I'm going to pass my yellow-belt test, I need a kung-fu-movie montage of me doing back falls in the sorrel flowers and meditating in the breeze and throwing dirt clods in the air and kicking them before they hit the ground.

Ruby and I head out barefoot. I've taken off my wig and crown. Her American-flag patch is sticking up again. She stops at the threshold on our way out the door, bows, and then laughs at herself. "Just wait. Next thing you know, you'll be bowing when you walk into a Walmart. It's just that we bow so *much*, you know?"

It's cooler outside than it's been in a while—only in the 80s. The crushed seashells in the driveway poke at our feet, and the long grass in the field makes that fresh, lettuce-y sound when we run through it. Ruby says, "OK, OK, but honestly—like, for real, wholeheartedly—there is a greater-than-0% chance that I am going to puke because I am, like, so full of dumplings right now."

I pick a sorrel flower and chew on the stem. She looks at me like I've just sprung snakes for hair.

I pick a flower for her. "Try it."

"No."

"Try it."

She wrinkles her nose.

"It's sour," I tell her. "But, you know, *good* sour. You don't eat it. You just chew on it. They say it's good for a stomachache."

"Who says that?"

"I don't know, *they* do."

She takes the flower from me, sniffs the torn stem, and bites into it. "Huh. That's actually decent."

"Told y—*Ack!*"

An ad starts playing on my glasses so suddenly and so loudly that it startles me. I'm not standing in a field anymore. I'm standing at the foot of a volcano, and the volcano is blowing up with blue-corn chips like *kaboom*, and the chips are raining down on me like ash.

I close the ad.

Ruby and I both laugh. She says, "It was the tornado, wasn't it? I got that one in the dentist chair, getting a filling. Pretty much the worst time for a jump-scare ad."

I pick up a dirt clod, toss it in the air, and try to hit it with kick five—the inside crescent kick, the smells-like-a-sushi-restaurant kick— but I miss. "So, what all's on the yellow-belt test anyway?"

Ruby's like, "Don't worry! It's easy! It's just your back fall and your side fall. And your first 10 basic kicks. And an escape from a straight wrist grab; an escape and two control techniques from a lapel grab; an escape and two control techniques from a high-collar grab; a strike, a control technique, and an escape from an elbow grab; and a strike, a control technique, and an escape from a shoulder grab."

"Oh, is *that* all?"

"It's not as bad as it sounds. It's all stuff you've practiced a million times in class already." She throws a dirt clod in the air, too, only when *she* tries to kick-five it, she makes contact, and the dirt clod explodes into a satisfying cloud of orange dust. There should be a jagged-edged comic-book bubble over her foot that says, "BANG!"

I applaud. I skip around her, waving my arms like a cheerleader. "Again!" I say. "Again!"

Kick six, the outside crescent kick, the smells-like-cutting-the-grass kick. *BOOM!*

Kick eight, the high heel front kick, the smells-like-Grandma's-cinnamon-gum-wrappers kick. *WHAM!*

Kicks I've never seen before. *SMACK! SLAM! KAPOW!* She kicks at dirt clods until she starts to get winded. Then she puts her hands on top of her head and forces herself to take slow, deep breaths.

And I'm like, "I can't believe what I just saw."

"Why?" Inhale. "You can"—exhale—"do it." Inhale. "It just"—exhale—"takes practice."

She brushes some of the orange dust from her foot and her leg. "You know," she says once her breathing has almost returned to normal, "I wonder if this is what it's like to do hapkido on Mars. The orange dirt, the haze. The wide-open space." She holds out both arms, as if she's trying to hug the field. Then she glances at me and puts her arms back down.

"What?" I say. "I can tell you want to say *something.*"

She shakes her head and stares at the spindly pine trees in the distance—beyond the field, beyond the rows of mobile homes, beyond the highway. "Sometimes I feel homesick," she says to the pines. "My mom says I've always been like that. She says I was born homesick." She looks at me. "Do you ever feel like that? Homesick?"

I remember sprinkling Callisto's food into her tank. I remember pressing thumbtacks into my walls—the walls our landlord let me paint teal—so I could hang my framed issues of *Mera.* I remember closing my closet door and hearing my stuffed peacock rattle, but I can't remember why I didn't bring the peacock with me. And I can't remember whether the thumbtacks were the plastic kind or the metal kind. And I know it's ridiculous to feel sad over thumbtacks. I know thumbtacks don't matter. But if I can't remember the thumbtacks today, what will I forget tomorrow? Will I forget whether my doorknob had a lock that you turn or a lock that you press? Will I forget how Callisto looked when she swam to the surface of the water to gobble up her food before it sank?

"Yeah," I say. "I do."

"Sometimes I ... This is going to sound crazy, OK? But sometimes I feel homesick for Mars even though I've never been there. I mean, *obviously* I've never been there. *Nobody* has been there—yet. But 'homesick' is still the best word I can use for the feeling. Just imagine being one of the first colonizers we send there—to have a whole planet to yourself, or almost to yourself. And you're constantly learning new things. And you get to spend your days—I mean, your *sols*; they call them *sols* there—you get to spend your sols tending to pea plants or cleaning the dust off of solar panels or singing 'The Wheels on the Bus' to the first native Martians. It all just sounds so ... so ..." She shrugs. "Maybe I just want to live a big life."

"I think *I* just want a quiet life. Big life, small life—doesn't matter as long as it's quiet. Because sometimes I sure do miss when things were quiet." I pick another piece of sorrel, break off most of the stem, and tuck the flower behind my ear. "But if anyone can have a big life on Mars, it's you."

She snorts. "They will *never* pick me to go to Mars."

"Who won't?"

"I don't know, *they* won't." She laughs and punches me in the arm—softly, but it's still like *ow*. "Anyway, that's all years and years in the future. After high school. And college. And more college. I have a lot to learn before I could even dream of standing one-thousandth of a chance of applying for the colonizer program and actually being chosen for it. It's not exactly an easy career."

"Yeah, you have a lot to learn about kids' songs."

"What?"

"The first Martian kids. They won't know what a bus is. They will have never *seen* a bus. So, it's got to be 'The Wheels on the *Rover* Go Round and Round.'"

We make up a few verses and sing them—"the camera on the rover goes click, click, click"; "the mole on the rover goes dig, dig, dig"—and then Ruby says, "OK, OK, so I have to brush up on children's songs. But you have to brush up on this."

She grabs my wrist. It startles me. She pulls me a few steps toward the edge of the field before I remember what to do: I make all of the muscles in my hand and fingers tense, I turn my body in the direction Ruby's thumb is pointing, and I slip out of her grip easily. Then I *kiyup* and throw a kick at her shin.

"Show off." She grins and grabs my lapel. "How about this?" She pulls me closer, close enough that I can see where her red lip pencil ends and her red lipstick begins. I force myself to look her in the eye. Today her eyeliner is glacier blue.

You know how, when you're driving on the highway with your windows down, the wind is like *wsssssssh*? But then, when you roll the windows up, it gets really quiet, really fast? And it's, like, the quietest quiet you've ever heard? Yeah. That's how I feel.

This time *she* breaks eye contact first. She lets go of my lapel. "Sorry, you don't know the twisted-lapel grab yet, do you? Just the straight-lapel grab."

"No, it's OK, I—"

"Here." She runs her fingers through her hair and moves to my side. She grabs the shoulder of my Mera gown. The sequins scratch against me through the cheap, thin fabric they're sewn onto. She looks straight ahead, across the sea of sorrel.

But I'm like, "No, it's OK, you can show me. What's twisted lapel? Show me."

"I can't. I mean, I *can't*." She does this *quit-it* gesture with her free hand. She glances at me and looks back at the sorrel real quick. "What I mean is, I can't teach you new stuff. Only Master Avery can do that. I can only help you with old stuff, if you ask me to help you. It's, like, a rule, you know?"

"OK, so we'll do the old lapel grab. Straight lapel or whatever it's called. Nothing new. Or, hey, we can do high-collar grab. Yeah. Let's do high-collar grab." I turn to face her. I move her hand from my shoulder to the back of my gown, where the zipper is. "Now what?"

This time she looks me in the eye, and *I'm* the one who looks away. I focus on the hollow of her throat instead. *Look up*, I tell myself. *Look up*. I fix my eyes on her lips again. They're soft-looking but not shiny, like an oil painting, and I make myself concentrate on whether she's wearing a coat of lip gloss over her lipstick or if her lipstick is just *like* that. If I don't concentrate on that—if I don't concentrate on *something*—I feel like I'm standing at the end of the high dive, staring down at the pool a million miles below, and I just can't take it.

Ruby loosens her grip on my costume. She rests her hand where my neck meets my shoulder. She says, "You tell me."

Yeah, I don't think we're talking about hapkido anymore.

I wonder if she used a top coat of lip balm, not lip gloss. I wonder if she blended it all together with a lipstick brush. Maybe blending would give her that oil-painting effect, and oh my God, what am I even doing right now? Why am I forcing myself to think about makeup?

I hold my breath and look her in the eye. *Just hug the ball tight and give a big push. What kind of push? A* biiig *push.*

I kiss her before I have time to think about it.

Only I guess I'm rushing so much that my aim is bad. I end up doing this half-kiss-on-the-lips, half-kiss-on-the-cheek thing. And once I realize that this kiss is a catastrophe, I pull away and want to undo it all—like, *Ctrl-Z! Ctrl-Z!* I'm afraid to see her reaction, so I look down at my feet. For some reason, I get hung up on the idea that I should really trim my toenails. Ruby's toenails are perfectly shaped and painted with polish that's iridescent like a dragonfly's wing. I notice that, too, only why? Like, really: *why?*

Ruby says, "Hey."

I wonder if she uses one of those foam things that you stick between your toes so the polish on one toenail doesn't get all over your other toes.

"Hey."

I wonder how long that nail polish lasts before it gets so chipped that she has to take it off. A week?

"Hey, where'd you go? Look up here."

Two weeks?

She leans closer to me, and OK, so, *this* is what a first kiss is supposed to feel like: like biting into a frozen grape; like slipping into bed when you've just shaved your legs, and your sheets have just been washed, and they still smell like detergent; like "ARE YOU FAT? WELL, YOU DON'T HAVE TO BE. BECAUSE WITH DR. TRUMAN'S MAGIC—"

I close the ad.

I laugh, and Ruby laughs, but I worry Ruby's laugh isn't a *good* laugh. It feels like a nervous laugh. Like a what-have-I-done? laugh. Like a why-did-I-say-"you too!"-when-the-waiter-said-"enjoy your lunch"? laugh. She folds her arms. There's a wrinkle between her eyebrows. She says we should probably head back.

And I say, "Yeah, sure, OK." But I don't feel like, *Yeah, sure, OK.* I feel like, *Do you regret what just happened? Are you trying to get away from me, like Ezra did? Are we still friends now? Or more than friends? What else did you tell Master Avery about me, besides that I'm very nice?*

We walk in silence until we're almost at the deck. "Wait." Ruby puts a hand out to stop me. "You've got my lipstick on your face." I wipe my lips on the back of my hand. She says I might have made it worse. My mouth looks even redder now.

I tell her I'm sure it's just red from all the rubbing, and it'll be back to normal here in a sec. But I'm making that up. I have no idea if it'll go back to normal. No one wearing lipstick has ever kissed me before. Other than Ruby and Ezra, *no one* has ever kissed me before.

She's like, "I should probably get home."

"Right."

"Because my parents might be wondering where I am."

"Right. Do you want me to hail you a ride?"

I'm already opening the rideshare app when she's like, "Let me say goodbye to your mom and grandma first." She laughs. She touches my wrist. What's going on? Does she like me, or does she *like*-like me? Just when I think I know, something changes. "Did you think I was going to just take off without saying anything to them?"

Maybe. Yes. "No."

When we step inside, the air conditioning feels as cold and delicious as walking down the freezer aisle at the grocery store, opening a door, and having all of that wonderful, white fog tumble out from the shelves of popsicles.

Grandma's still asleep. Mom's standing over her, looking down at her daisy tattoo. The pedals are pool-water blue, bluer than I've ever seen them before. Mom grabs her by the shoulders and shakes her, and her head kind of lolls from side to side.

Ruby looks at me like, *what's going on?*

And I'm like, "Her sugar's low. She's diabetic. I should help her," but I just stand there, staring.

"I've got some Starburst in my backpack," Ruby says. "She can have those. I mean, they're practically 90% sugar. I already ate all the red and yellow ones. They're my favorites. But I'm sure she won't mind being stuck with the pink and orange ones—"

"That's a great idea," Mom says over her shoulder. "Go get her backpack, Louisa."

"She got first place in the rodeo before. Or third place. I don't know. There's a trophy, and—"

"*Louisa*. Go get her backpack."

# CHAPTER 22

I don't know how Grandma can sleep in this hospital room. It's bright. It's loud. She's hooked up to an IV and a bunch of beeping, flashing things. She's got the TV blaring a bowling tournament, and every few seconds, pins explode. But somehow, with all of that, she's managed to nod off.

There's one chair in the room—an orange, plastic one with screws in the back that my hair keeps getting stuck on—and Mom and I are taking turns sitting in it.

It's Mom's turn in the chair. "I'm mad at her," she whispers. "Is it OK that I'm mad at her?"

And I'm like, "Mad at who?" even though I already know the answer.

She nods toward Grandma. "I'm mad at her because this is the result of decades of bad choices. The whole time I was growing up, there'd be doctors telling her to check her sugar and eat better and at least *try* to exercise—like, bruh, take a walk once in a while, you know?—but I swear to God, it was Willy Wonka's chocolate factory all the time. And *she knew*. I mean, *she knew* not to do that. She knew it could cause all these health problems down the line, but it's like she didn't care. Or she didn't care enough. It's like she didn't care that one day I'd have to uproot my life to take care of her." I want to remind her that the hurricane is what uprooted her life—not Grandma—but I keep my mouth shut. "And did you know she used to smoke? Like, actual cigarettes? That was a whole nother thing altogether. And the doctors would tell her, 'Sarah, you should really try to give these cigarettes up because they make you more likely to have a stroke. They make you more likely to have a heart attack. And you want to live long enough to see your daughter graduate, don't you? And if she has kids one day, you want to be able to play with your grandchildren, right?' Huh." Mom snorts. "Well, other than trying that nicotine gum for a while, she—"

"Ssssh," I say because Grandma's waking up now. She blinks at the ceiling. She blinks at me.

She tries to sit up, but Mom says *no, no, stay down now; lie down; just lie down.* And she does, but she starts pulling at her IV, and Mom's like, *you've got to leave that alone.*

Grandma picks at the tape that's holding the IV to the back of her hand. She mumbles something. Mom leans closer to her. She mumbles again.

Mom clicks her tongue. "Don't be ridiculous. You're not going to die." To *me* she says, "Let's switch." She stands up and motions for me to sit in the chair.

Grandma wiggles her feet under the blanket. She's looking more awake now. "But, I mean, what if I *die*-die?" She tries to kick the end of the blanket off of her feet, but it's tucked under the mattress, so she gives up. "What if I die while I'm thinking of something stupid?"

"Look, Mom. Listen. The whole reason— seriously, Louisa, sit down; you're making me nervous, pacing around like that—the whole reason you're here is so you *won't* die. That's what the doctors are here for, all right? You're not going to die. You're not."

But I'm like, "Leave me alone. I'm trying not to tic out, OK?" I shake my hands in the air like I just rinsed them, and there aren't any towels, and I need to get the water off.

And Mom's like, "That's what your therapist told you to do? To walk around like that?"

I slump into the chair. "No." I sit on my hands. *100 ... 99 ...* On TV, somebody picks up a seven-ten split. *98 ... 97 ...*

When I get to 53, the urge goes away. I say, "Besides, Grandma, if it gets bad enough, the doctors can operate on you to keep you alive."

Mom looks at me like *why would you say something like that?*

I look at her like *why wouldn't I?*

"But what if I die while they're operating on me?" Grandma says. She picks at the tape some more. "It happens, you know. It happens." I tell her to forget I said anything. I don't know what I'm talking about; I'm just a kid. Forget it. But she says, "It does happen though. I ought to know. Did I ever tell you how I almost died in surgery before?"

Mom's eyebrows shoot up. "What?"

"When I was having *you*."

Mom stares at her.

"Oh, yeah. Didn't I tell you? I must have told you. They didn't want me to have a baby at all—because of my diabetes, *you* know—and do you know what else? The very day I married your dad, I was sitting at the beauty salon, and they were doing my hair up for the wedding, with baby's breath and all that. And everybody was talking about how I wouldn't ever be able to have a baby, and oh, isn't it so sad. And my mom was there, getting her hair done up, too, right? Well, my sugar got real low, and I broke out in a terrible sweat. Just terrible, terrible. The hairdresser had to get me some orange juice real quick, and my mom had to hold it up so I could drink it. 'Drink your juice, Sarah. Drink your juice.'"

"Mom, that's not your life. That's the plot of *Steel Magnolias*."

"But I didn't listen to them. No, they couldn't tell *me* what to do. But when I had you, it was a C-section because—"

"Hold on," I say. "What's *Steel Magnolias*?"

Mom tells me I have to know what *Steel Magnolias* is.

I shake my head.

"*Steel Magnolias.* Bruh, we *just* watched the new remake."

I have no memory of this. Like, none. Is this what it's like to have dementia? Does Grandma feel like this all the time? I shake my head again.

Mom rolls her eyes. "You know that red-velvet cake I make that's shaped like an armadillo?"

"Oh, God, not the bleeding one."

"Yeah. That one. That's from *Steel Magnolias.* It's this old movie your Grandma loves. It's set in—Mom, stop picking at your IV. It's set in—I *said* quit picking at it."

Grandma pulls the tape a third of the way off.

"You're not going to—Mom, leave that thing alone, I said. You're not going to die. The doctors here—"

*"Big Mac, McDLT, a Quarter Pounder with some cheese, Filet-O-Fish, a hamburger, a cheeseburger, a Happy Meal—"*

On my glasses, I pull up the old video of her in the rodeo. "Hey, Grandma."

*"McNuggets, tasty golden French fries, regular or larger sizes—"*

*"Grandma."* I hand her my glasses. "Look what I found."

She puts on my glasses and smiles. She sinks down into her pillows. "Is that—? That's Angel. That's me and Angel."

"Do you remember this race?" I ask.

"We had lockers there. Mine was number ten. Kept a mirror on it with this frame made out of braided rope and pony beads. Pony beads don't look like ponies, though. They're just plain plastic, in all different colors. I don't know why they call them that. Anyway. Nobody ever used the locker next to mine, but it had a Post-It on it that said 'It's Working,' and nobody ever told me why the Post-It was there or what it meant, but one day, the Post-It was just gone, and Jesus Christ, what if I die without ever knowing what that Post-It was all about and what was working and why anybody should care that it was working?"

"Hey, Grandma, don't—"

"I'm so tired."

"Don't cry over a Post-It. Here. Here, look at this." I start up an app on my glasses that makes you feel like you're at a rodeo. Hooves thud, dust flies, a mariachi band plays, a crowd yells, and Grandma loves it all, right? She's looking around and pointing and saying things like, "Seven-and-a-half seconds!" and "Here come the rodeo clowns!" And maybe she's not as bad off as I think. Maybe now that she ate those Starburst, and she's on an IV, and she's got doctors and nurses checking on her, everything will go back to normal.

"What do you see now?" I ask her.

"Bull riding. Always was one of my favorite events to watch. So—Oh, I think I know this guy. I think this is Josh. Yeah, this is Josh." She waves. "Hey, Josh! Joshy Boy!"

Whoever Josh is, this can't be him. This is a bull rider that the software put together out of thousands vaguely Josh-like bull riders. But I'm like, "Oh, yeah? Josh is there, huh? Was Josh your friend? Tell me about Josh."

"I want to go talk to him. Will it let me go talk to him? *Hey, Josh!*"

"You can't—Grandma, don't get up. The doctor said you've got to stay in bed. And, anyway, I don't think the app will—"

"*Joshy Boy!*"

"You've got to lie back down. The doctor said—"

"Don't touch me, little girl."

"Sorry. I didn't mean to. I just need my glasses back for a—"

"I *said* don't *touch* me." She grabs my wrist. You know that bony bump on the back of your wrist? Grandma is squeezing mine so hard that the seahorse charm on my bracelet is crushing it, and I'm like, this is what a boiled peanut feels like right before you crack it open.

I'm about to apologize again when, out of the corner of my eye, I see something move. Before I know what I'm doing—before I even know what it is that I'm seeing—I've blocked her slap. Or her punch. It's hard to tell which because her hand isn't really flat or a fist. It's just kind of *there*. I *kiyup*, too. I think that startles her: it makes her blink. And I think it startles Mom, too, because she gasps and goes "ah!" and presses the call button for the nurse.

I pull my wrist free from Grandma's grasp, the same way I practiced it with Ruby in the field. Then I step out into the hall while Mom says, "Okaaay. Okaaay. Let's take some deeeep breaths."

I lean back against the wall and start to text Ruby about what happened before I remember my glasses aren't on. A janitor rumbles past me—pushing a cart of cleaning supplies—and it's weird to feel the breeze he kicks up against my whole face, even around my eyes. Normally my glasses block that.

No arrows are glowing on the floor. No ads are telling me to buy a bouquet from the gift shop or a cup of ice from the cafeteria. I have no idea where I am or where I should go or how I got here from the car. When I sit on a bench that's the color of boiled cabbage and start to tic out, I can't use face-ID to guess the names of people who stare at me and think, "Well, what do you expect from an Aries?" or

"OK, sure, I may have Tourette's, but at least I don't have a reason to buy anal cream."

So, I cross my arms, stare at a point on the floor where four tiles meet, try to tune out the beeps and pings and voices around me, and imagine I'm doing kick nine, the axe kick, the squeezing-Play-Doh-through-a-potato-ricer kick; I'm breaking someone's wrist when they grab my collar; I'm slicing someone in the liver when they grab my shoulder; I'm pulling my shirt from someone's grasp, and I'm running, running, running.

# CHAPTER 23

Ruby has beanbag chairs that look like partially deflated planets. I'm sitting on her bed with my feet propped up on Jupiter. "Isn't this the song from that suspenders commercial?" I ask.

"Yeah, but you've got to hear the whole thing," Ruby says, turning it up:

*Take a look at the lawman*

*Beating up the wrong guy.*

*Oh, man, wonder if he'll ever know*

*He's in the best-selling show.*

*Is there life on Mars?*

I smile. "You just like it because it has Mars in it."

She shoves my feet off of Jupiter. "No! It's good! It's really, actually, truly good!"

*It's on America's tortured brow*

*That Mickey Mouse has grown up a cow.*[i]

I groan. I'm about to say we should play something that *isn't* a hundred-year-old rock song when Ruby's little sister barges into the room. She turns her toes out, bends her knees like a ballerina, stands up straight again, and puts her arms over her head. "Y'all want to hear a joke?" She twirls. "What has ears but doesn't hear?"

"You?" Ruby mutters.

"Corn!" Tally says, twirling again. Then: "Hey, guess what I have? A trampoline." Twirl. "And guess what else? A lizard. You want to see it, Louisa?" Twirl.

I don't know if she means the trampoline or the lizard. "Um, sure?"

Ruby turns off the music. "Leave us alone, Tally."

"I'm going to go get my lizard."

"I said, leave us alone, Tally."

"My lizard's name is Lizzie." She flounces out of the room. Ruby calls after her to close the door, but she doesn't. Laughter floats in from somewhere else in the house. Somebody says something about hummus, which makes people laugh even harder, and I can't even imagine why because hummus? Really?

Ruby closes her door hard enough to make the clapper pad that's hanging from the doorknob go *thwap*.

"They never shut up." She sits back down next to me. "I know that sounds mean, and I'm sorry, I really am, because they're all nice people, and there's really nothing wrong with them, but honestly, they never stop talking. Every year I spend most of Samhain holed up in here, playing Nintendo or watching something on my glasses or practicing kicks or listening to music or doing anything that involves not being out there with them. It's not so bad once they get the fire started"—the fire? what fire?—"because at least then we're outside, and there's room to breathe and move and stuff. And Dad gets out his guitar, and everybody starts to write down what they want to leave behind in the New Year so they can throw the paper in the fire and, like, *visualize*. But until then, ugh. Talk, talk, talk. But, hey! That reminds me! I wanted to show you my short stick, with the sigil on it."

While she opens the trunk at the foot of her bed, I look at the "40 Basic Judo Throws" poster on the back of her door. I've heard of some of the throws—like *o goshi*, the major hip throw, and *o soto gari*, the major outer reaping throw—but there are a ton of other throws I've never even heard of, like the body-drop throw, which sounds like a special ability somebody would unlock in one of the play-throughs Grandma watches. Four round stickers that look like moons hold the poster to the door— one at each corner.

Ruby's still rummaging through her trunk when a news story about Tropical Storm Theta—way off in the Atlantic somewhere— takes over my glasses. As soon as the tie-dye-looking map swirls across my lenses, I close it. Now an ad starts up, and I'm standing at a counter, and a smiling woman in a red-and-yellow visor is like, "Welcome back to McDonald's, Louisa! Something tells me you're in the mood for a chocolate soft-serve cone with chocolate-covered-cricket topping right about now." Did ... did that woman just *wink* at me? "No problem. We've all been there." This all sounds weirdly familiar. Have I had this talk before? I swear, these ads are always listening in on our conversations and stealing parts of them. They *say* they don't, but they totally do. "Don't worry, Louisa. Here at McDonald's, PMS just stands for 'Positive McDonald's Smile.'"

Good Lord. *Close.*

Ruby finds her short stick. "I was scared there for a second. Thought I'd lost it." She hands the stick to me. "So, sigils are these secret symbols for, like, whatever you wish would happen. My parents carved this one into my short stick as kind of a good-luck thing. It means, 'I move like water.' It's got most of the consonants worked into it—so, *M, V, L,* and *K*—but also this water shape?" There's a jagged line, like if you were doodling water on the back of an envelope. I trace it with my index finger. "Anyway, it's all really sweet of them, but it's also kind of embarrassing?"

"I like it! It's thoughtful!" I hand it back to her. While she puts it away, I ask about the stickers holding up the judo poster.

She says they're Jupiter's biggest moons. She points to each one as she names it: Europa, Ganymede, Io, Callisto. And I'm like, "Callisto!"

And I tell her how I never knew what it really looked like because everything I know about space I learned from Mera comics. And I tell her about burying Callisto, and how there was a shovel in the bed of the truck the whole time, only I don't mention Ezra or his moms at all. I accidentally-on-purpose make it sound like the truck was ours. And I tell her about the fishpond at the sushi restaurant, and the way the sushi restaurant smelled like fives. And I didn't even mean to tell her any of that stuff, but hey, now it's out there.

I expect Ruby to give me a that's-weird squint, but she doesn't. She just sits next to me and says, "Sounds like synesthesia to me."

"What?"

"Synesthesia. It's when one sense—"

Blam. The door flies open. Tally stands in the doorway, holding a little habitat with a lizard, a friendship bracelet, and a stick in it. "This is Lizzie. She's my lizard."

Ruby mumbles, "You said that already."

"You want to hold her?"

"Nobody wants to hold your lizard, Tally."

"No, no, it's OK. My mom had a lizard like Lizzie once. A green anole named Emerald."

Tally flumps next to us on the bed. She unclicks the lid of the habitat. "This is for when Lizzie travels. Her real house is in my room. Do you want to see it later? Do you want to see my room? I have my own Nintendo like Ruby's now. Do you want to see it? Hey. Hey! Do you want to hear a joke?"

She sets Lizzie in my hand. Lizzie blinks at me.

Tally doesn't wait for me to say whether I want to hear the joke or not. "A man went to the zoo. All they had on exhibit was a dog. It was a Shih Tzu."

Ruby tells her to go play Fantasticats. Watch *Frozen 4* again. *Something.*

But from somewhere else in the house, Ruby's dad is like, "Ruby, stop having your sister tell that joke. It's inappropriate." Somebody out there—probably the hummus person—finds that hilarious. *Ha! Ha! Ha!*

"I didn't. She just came in here and, like, told it. And like I said before, I'm not the one who taught her that joke. And she doesn't even get the joke, I promise."

"I do so get it!"

Ruby looks at me. "She doesn't get it."

Now their mom gets involved: "Tally, come here, kiddo."

"No!"

"Tally, just come here. I want you to help me do something."

Tally folds her arms. She glares at the wall. Lizzie is, by now, standing on my shoulder.

"You want to help us toast the pumpkin seeds?" their dad asks.

"What?"

Ruby rolls her eyes. "He said, 'Do you want. To help. Them toast. The pumpkin seeds?'"

Tally stops glaring. "Can I do the cinnamon?"

Her dad yells back: "What did you say?"

"*Can I do the cinnamon?*"

"Sure, you can do the cinnamon!"

Tally smiles, scoops up Lizzie, and puts her back in her habitat.

I tell Ruby that eights smell like cinnamon. She says that's awesome.

Tally clips the lid back on the habitat. "Bye!" Then zoom. She and Lizzie are gone.

Ruby closes her door. Again.

"Anyway," she plops next to me, "synesthesia. It's when one sense gets tied up with another sense. So like, for example, there are people who associate numbers with certain colors. Like, maybe threes always feel red or sixes always feel green. That kind of thing. Here. *OK, Glazier: What is synesthesia?*" And the next thing I know, she and I are each watching the same synesthesia video—a video where a cellist talks about how B-flats look golden, and a math major talks about how eights are jolly— and I'm pointing at my lenses and saying things like "That's it!" and "Exactly!" and Ruby is saying things like "See?" and "Right?"

"You know," I say, "this is a lot better than when I told my boyfriend about it. He said I have an atypical brain. I mean, he's ... we started dating, but I had to move away."

"Oh! You had a boyfriend? That's ... yeah, that's cool. Did he move away, too, or ... ?"

"No, he stayed back home. He and his moms are rebuilding."

"Oh."

"I mean, not because of me. He moved because of—"

"Right."

"The storm."

"Right, right."

There's a pause, and I say, "Hurricane Louisa," for no reason except to fill it. "Yup. Hurricane Louisa."

Ruby winds the pillow tag around her finger. She's like, "Everybody's got *something*."

"What do you mean?"

"I mean, everybody's got *something* that makes them atypical. You've got your synesthesia—"

"And my Tourette's," I mutter.

"Yeah, OK, but did you know that Master Avery has depression? To give, like, just one example? She's talked about it in class before. That's part of why she started learning hapkido in the first place—to help her mood—and she still takes meds for it. She's talked about that, too. The medication."

"Oh, nobody cares about depression. Who *doesn't* have depression? It's like the heat exhaustion of mental illnesses. Everybody's had it."

"Fine. Well, I've got anxiety—"

"Everybody's had that, too," I say, trying to sound calmer than I am. "And at least with anxiety ... I mean, I know anxiety can be bad. I'm not saying it's easy or anything like that. But you're lucky that people at your school don't mimic your anxiety symptoms to make fun of you, and nobody avoids you in the grocery store when your anxiety's acting up. Acting ᵘᵖ. Anxiety's acting ᵘᵖ." I sigh. "Sorry. Sometimes talking about my tics makes me, like, *have* tics. It makes me have ᵗⁱᶜˢ." I sit on my hands. "Wow. I can't believe it. I just tic-ed over the word 'tic.'"

"Think about Charlotte's chair," she says. "Not everybody has one of *those*. And it's, like, this super obvious thing, right? But nobody thinks badly of Charlotte because of it. I mean, Charlotte could annihilate me in a fight if she wanted to, and I outrank her in hapkido. And she does leather working. She makes all her own purses. She even sells some of them. She sings, too. Did you know that? She's in a chorus and everything. Trust me: *no one* thinks Charlotte is weird."

I sigh. "I guess."

"And what about your grandma? She has dementia, but—"

"And diabetes. And nerve damage."

"But she still seems to enjoy being alive. She likes her pet fish. And she likes spending time with you. And didn't you say she likes wearing your glasses? Here. You should show her this sometime. She'd love it." Ruby sends me an app called Yurika. For the second or two that it's downloading, I'm trying to force myself to tell her about Ezra—to clarify that he's my boyfriend now, today, at this actual moment— but soon she's saying, "*OK, Glazier: Turn on the stars*. Now you do it."

"Um, *OK, Glazier: Turn on the stars?*"

Her ceiling—which I hadn't even looked at before because unless you're in a cathedral, who looks at a ceiling—lights up with white freckles. Then Ruby turns off the regular overhead light, and it's like *surprise! You're in an RV commercial!* Because there are one bajillion individual stars. No clouds, no light pollution—just stars. Some are as bright as laser pointers. Some are faint, like the pinpricks of light that come through your T-shirt if you pull the collar over your head. Some seem as close as kick one, the shin kick. Some seem as far away as kick ten, the front thrust heel kick, done in the flying style.

And I'm like, "I ... wow."

And she's like, "Right?"

I look for the only two constellations I can ever find: Orion and the Big Dipper. And that must be the North Star that the handle of the Big Dipper is pointing to. I try to find Leo, but I don't really know what I'm looking for, so I give up.

"*Déjà vu,*" I say.

"What?"

"I feel like I've done this before, but I know I haven't. I mean, I'm sure I haven't. At least, I think I'm sure. I've never seen anything quite like ... well, like *this* before." I wave my arm to indicate the whole visible universe. "I guess this is what the sky used to look like every night, before we all had electricity."

"If you turned off all the lights everywhere in the world, and if you erased all of the clouds, this is what the sky would have looked like on the night I was born, if you stood in this exact spot. April 24, 2035."

"Seriously?"

"What's your birthday?"

"No, no, but seriously?"

"Seriously." She laughs. "What's your birthday?"

"August 10, 2036."

"*OK, Glazier: Show the stars at this location on August 10, 2036.*"

The night sky creeps across Ruby's ceiling. On one end of the room, stars keep colliding with the place where the ceiling joins the wall and disappearing. On the other end of the room, new stars keep crowding in. I feel a little dizzy until the sky stops moving. Once the sky settles down, we stare at it without saying anything. Then Ruby says, real quiet, "Happy birthday." And my heart feels like it's going to expand out of my chest like over-proofed dough ballooning out of a loaf pan.

Her pinky finger hooks itself around mine in the dark. I swear I can hear my pulse in my ears. I should look at her, but I can't look at her, because if I look at her, I'm pretty sure I'll pass out. I keep gazing at the stars on her ceiling. I scoot closer to her until our arms are pressed against each other.

I'm trying to talk myself into grabbing her hand and holding it properly when the door bangs open and light pollution pours in from the hallway, and Tally's like, "*Beef!*"

Ruby jerks her hand away from mine. She throws the galaxy pillow at Tally. "Get out of here, go away, what's the matter with you?"

"*Beeeeef!*"

"Get out of here, what are you even doing right now?" She throws a pillow at her that looks like the moon—or *a* moon. "Dad! Tell Tally to get out of here."

"It's the Beef Game. If you want to play, all you do is say 'beef.' *Beeeeef! Beef beef beeeeef!*"

Her dad yells from somewhere else in the house: "Tally! Come help me do the cinnamon!"

"Bye!" She runs out of the room, yelling *beef* down the hall.

Ruby gets up and closes the door again. She turns the light back on, and after we're done squinting and going "Ugh!" and "Aaah!" because it's so bright, she's like, "Yeah, so I guess we're done with the stars for now?" as she tosses the pillows back onto the bed.

But I'm like, "No! No, we don't have to be, let's look at the sky on some other day. Is it just stars? Is it planets, too? Can we look at Jupiter's moons? Oh! Can we look at Callisto?"

Ruby grins. She kills the lights. She sits back down next to me. *"OK, Glazier: Show me Callisto."*

I say the same thing. A moon that looks like a disco ball in a dim room floats toward me.

"Whatever I *thought* Callisto would look like, it was nothing like this. This is really ... really ..."

"Yeah. It's really *really*. The sticker on my door doesn't do it justice." She takes a deep breath. "Hey. So. This." Out of the corner of my eye, I can see her point at herself, at me, and back again. "What do you think about *this*?" She doesn't look away from Callisto, though. Neither do I. Why are we both acting like it's impossible to look at each other? You'd think we were avoiding looking straight at a solar eclipse.

"What do I *think* about it?"

"Yeah. I mean, if you *have* thought about it. Because *I've* thought about it. And *I* think it could be, you know"—she takes another deep breath—"good. But what do *you* think about it?"

I twist my charm bracelet around my wrist. "What do *I* think about it?"

Now, look: I'm not an idiot. I know this would be the most movie-ish moment to tell her she makes me feel like there's a pinwheel in my chest, and somebody's blowing on it, and it's going *thwap thwap thwap*. I should take her hand. I should kiss her. But all I say is, "That guy Ezra?"

"Who?"

"That guy. Ezra. The guy who called my brain atypical."

The mattress moves; I can feel her shift away from me. "Your ex-boyfriend?"

"Yeah. Sort of."

"Oh."

"I mean, I'm over him." I try to sound more convincing: "Like, *totally* over him." But am I? "We're not together anymore." What am I saying? Of course we are. "Because he likes this other girl. Named Lydia." Stop talking. "They're in this illustration club together, or something, and he's always talking about her." Shut up, shut up, shut up. "He drew a picture of me as Mera, but that was forever ago. And since then, he drew Lydia in this whole *other* picture, which he left at my house—I mean, at Grandma's house—and the entire reason he was even over there is that my Grandma started that fire and his moms had to come clean up the mess."

"*He's* always talking about Lydia?"

"What?"

"Ezra. Your boyfriend. You said *he's* always talking about this other girl. You didn't say *he was*. So, you still talk to him?"

"I ... it's complicated." Somewhere, a cork pops. The loud laugher laughs again. *HA! HA! HA!* I repeat myself: "It's compli<sup>cated</sup>."

"Oh. Well." She picks at a hangnail. "I mean, *I* was just wondering if you wanted to keep practicing hapkido with me. I was thinking you could, like, come over more often so we could practice our, you know, holds."

"Oh."

"Because it can be hard to practice those on your own."

"Oh."

"And we can practice our throws, too. Because it's not like it does me any good to throw Tally around. She's too little for it to count. I mean, I could totally wreck a throw, right? Like, I could have the wrong posture, or I could leave too much space between us, and she'd still go flying. Because with someone your own size, if you do a throw wrong, it'll feel difficult, but if you get everything right—the timing, the positioning, *everything*—it feels effortless."

"Right."

"Because that's all *I* was talking about."

"Right. Yeah, definitely. Absolutely." Now I *do* look at her face in the dark, trying to tell if she's buying any of this.

She's looking at me, probably trying to tell if *I'm* buying any of this.

Unless this was all a big misunderstanding. Maybe she really was just talking about throws and holds. *What do you think about* this? *I think it could be good.* Maybe "it" just meant "practice."

So, I'm like, "Ezra isn't any help. He lives back home, so he can't practice with me," which isn't a lie. "You should see his drawing of a roundhouse kick. You'd break your foot if you did it like that. And, hey, the one time I did try to practice with him—when his moms were fixing our kitchen—he was a big baby about it. He was practically crying." OK, I kind of embellished that last part.

Ruby's like, "Then let's practice, you and me. Aren't you testing soon?"

"In, like, two weeks or something, yeah."

"Did Master Avery tell you what happens at graduation? She'll have you demonstrate some technique or another. When I got my yellow belt, she had me show off some of my kicks, but really, it's different for everyone. Some people do escapes. Some people do falls." She gets up and takes the kick pad from her doorknob. She smacks it once, hard, and holds it straight out. "Show me kick five."

The smell of wasabi and soy sauce. The snap of conjoined chopsticks being pulled apart before you use them. The shattering of fortune cookies when you break them open. *You are destined to find romance after the procedure.*

From the other side of the door: *HA! HA! HA!*

I kick the pad so hard it flies out of her hand and bangs against the wall.

She picks it up, wraps the strap around her wrist this time, and holds the pad in front of her shin. "Kick one."

*Slam.*

She holds it close to the ground. "Kick nine."

As I bring my heel down on it, a text from Mom appears on my lenses: "Everything's fine." Oh no. *Slam.* "Grandma's going into surgery." Ruby holds the pad in front of her chest, like a shield, for kick ten. "They've got to amputate."

Ruby smacks the pad again. "Front thrust heel kick," she says. "Right here. Right in the solar plexus."

Mom texts, "They say they'll amputate below the knee."

"Louisa?" Ruby says.

"They say the infection is spreading too fast."

"Louisa? Hey, Louisa, you OK?"

# CHAPTER 24

This time I put my hair up in a bun so it won't get stuck in the chair when it's my turn to sit in it. Because it's a different chair, in a different room, but they're all the same chair, really—the same screws, the same hair-pulls.

Mom says, "This place is quieter than a library full of mimes"—even though it isn't; even though we can hear people talking at the nurses' station and machines beeping everywhere—"so I've had it. I'm turning on the TV. What do you want to watch? Stop me when you see something that looks good."

A cop shining a flashlight into a dark room.

Sauce being ladled onto a pizza crust.

A hen fighting off a cat that wants to eat her chicks.

A roulette wheel spinning.

A tree falling over.

I say, "You sounded like her just then."

"Like who?"

"The thing about the mimes. That sounded like something *she* would say." I glance toward Grandma, who's asleep in her hospital bed.

"Oh," Mom says. "Huh."

A man steaming the wrinkles out of a wedding dress.

A woman shuffling cards.

A cat scratching in its litter box.

Basil leaves being torn and sprinkled over a different pizza than before.

Mom says, "She asked if she could keep the leg."

"No way."

"Really."

"No *way.*"

"I'm being serious."

"Can—"

"No, Louisa, she can't keep the leg."

Mom turns the TV off and sighs. We both stare at the space where the bottom third of

Grandma's leg would be under the covers if Grandma still *had* the bottom third of her leg.

On my glasses, I read some of the texts she's sent me: "Take a deep breath." "There's an app for everything." "SHUT UP AND TALK TO HER." I pull up the memory of her in the pet store, holding bags and bags of fish. I hear her call Ezra insincere while she lies next to me on the kitchen floor. I listen as she tells me about the fish tank she had in her bathroom, back when she lived in the sunflower house. I play back the video of her competing in the rodeo— leaning forward, ponytail flying. I watch her walking down the driveway to welcome us to our new home. And I see her at last Thanksgiving, standing with her frog collection on the deck, wearing her patent-leather shoes, waving goodbye.

I tend to forget my glasses are always recording this stuff. Unlike Grandma—and unlike me—they remember everything. The big moments. The small moments. The moments that seemed small at the time, but when you look back on them, you realize they were actually the biggest moments of all, and you should have paid more attention to them when you had the chance.

# CHAPTER 25

Grandma's face appears on my lenses. I know it isn't real—the way the burned hair I smell when I see a number one isn't real—but I still make eye contact with her when I say, "*OK, Grandma: Should I break up with Ezra?*"

This time, Glazier's voice doesn't tell me the answer. Grandma's does. "Why are you asking me questions you already know the answer to?"

"That's not helpful."

"Sure it is. You already know what *I* think: he's insincere; he's shallow; he's dumber than a sea cucumber; he's dumber than a *cucumber-*cucumber. But what do *you* think?"

"I don't know what I think. That's why I'm asking you."

"Oh, please. Of *course* you know what you think. You just don't want to admit it."

I take the stuffed moose off of my closet door and squeeze its crinkly body. I shake it to hear it rattle.

*"OK, Grandma: Give me more advice about Ezra."*

"You should date someone who makes you feel like every day is your birthday, and you're in a Mexican restaurant, and all the waiters are singing to you, and they bring you fried iced cream with a sparkler stuck in it, for free."

"What is that supposed to mean?"

"Why are you asking me questions you already know the answer to?"

*"Ugh."* I shake the moose so hard that its antlers flap back and forth. "This app is the worst."

"Hey, it's not *the app's* fault that Ezra makes you feel like someone's following you around with a kazoo."

I sigh. "This is hard, Grandma. Why do relationships have to be so hard?"

*"Pffft.* They don't. If you're with the right person, the relationship is easy."

"So, it's like a throw," I say. "If you try to throw someone, and it's really hard to do, you're going about it all wrong, but if you do it right, it's effortless. At least, it's *supposed* to feel effortless."

"Exactly. So, the real question isn't 'why do relationships have to be so hard?' The real question is 'who do you feel easy with?'"

"I don't know who I feel easy with."

"Yeah. Uh-huh."

"I don't."

"Sure."

"*I don't!*"

Grandma starts singing the suspenders-commercial song, only she does it in a mariachi style, and she's wearing a sombrero now, and somehow there's a guitar and a violin and a trumpet accompanying her:

*"It's a God-awful small affair*

*To the girl with the mousy hair."*

I'm like, "This is making me distinctly uncomfortable. *OK, Grandma: Off,*" but she keeps going:

*"But her mummy is yelling, 'No,'*

*And her daddy has told her to go."*

*"OK, Grandma: I get it. I get it. Stop. I'll tell him. I'll break up with Ezra, OK?"*

And I decide that I'll call him. Because I can't tell him in person. I mean, obviously. I'll plan everything I want to say, write it down, and talk to him when we both have time for a good, long chat—like two adults. Because that's all it is: a chat. Just like every other time we've talked since I moved. Not awkward at all.

# CHAPTER 26

I start to text Ezra, "Should we break up?"

But then I delete it because I don't want to know the answer. Except Grandma—or quote-unquote "Grandma"—was right: I already know the answer. It's like when someone hears thunder and gasps and goes, "Was that thunder?" Or when you're sitting there with a sandwich in your mouth, and somebody goes, "Having a sandwich?"

Huh. A sandwich sounds good.

I head to the kitchen, where Mom is throwing away all the stale burger buns, expired baked beans, sticky jars of applesauce, and moth-infested flour. Pretty soon, there will be nothing in the cabinet but an unopened jar of Tony Chachere's Cajun seasoning and a bottle of vinegar with a jalapeño floating in it. The trash can that's next to her is full of wrappers, bags, cans, boxes, and an ooze that is honestly kind of worrying.

She holds up her hand like *stop!* "I'm on a roll," she says. "Give me a minute."

I look around. "Where's the frog with the dish sponge in its mouth?"

"Threw it away. Nasty." She tosses a box of probably-pebble-hard raisins in the trash.

"What about the rooster towel?"

"Threw it away. Nasty. All frayed and stained and whatever."

"Why are you doing all this at nine o'clock at night, though? Are you, like, OK? Or what?"

She ignores my questions and hands me a box of trash bags. "If you want to be helpful, you can clean out some of the stuff that your Grandma left in your room. Like those puzzles with missing pieces, and those concert-ticket stubs. Those can go. Well, on second thought, maybe not the ticket stubs. But ... oh, I don't even know anymore."

I stand there, staring at the box of trash bags until my glasses tell me where I can order six boxes of them for the price of twelve, and why I should feel guilty for using disposable trash bags instead of reusable ones made from recycled water bottles, and why Leos like me should buy Lionheart-brand reusable trash bags because Lionheart honors the lion within. Then a lion leaps into my field of vision, and I jump, and the lion slinks away, and Mom says, "That Reba McEntire shirt—do you think she'll wear it at The Harbor? I don't think she'll wear it. I mean, I've never seen her wear it before. Have you?"

"What's she going to say when she comes back, though, and we've gotten rid of her stuff?"

"Louisa, you act like we're cleaning out her house or something." That is literally what we're doing. "We're just downsizing. We're minimizing. Sublimating."

"Sublimating?"

"Yeah, sublimating. It's a way of getting rid of all the possessions you don't need anymore, only it's, like, spiritual. It's this whole *thing* now. Here, I saw this great video about it. Let me—"

"Don't send me the video, Mom."

"No, it's short! It's only, like, a minute long."

"Do *not* send me the video."

"But it's just—"

"I'm going! I'm going!"

I run to my room and close the door behind me. I glance around at the Reba McEntire T-shirt; the 2-D printer; the jigsaw puzzles; the pink, plastic toolbox full of screwdrivers and hammers and wrenches with pink, plastic handles; the pile of half-used eyeshadow compacts, the barrel-racing trophy, the PlayStation box that has everything but a PlayStation inside of it.

I set the trophy on my bed. I know Grandma will want to keep that. I throw the puzzles away because Mom's right—they've got to all be missing pieces by now—and The Harbor probably has a ton of puzzles for people to borrow. Don't places like that always have tons of puzzles? I open the PlayStation box behind the puzzles, salvage the rodeo ribbon and the Clint Black ticket stub out of it, and put everything else in the trash bag because nobody actually uses those single buttons, do they? And who knows how old these glasses are? And this receipt is for some groundcherry-flavored Pop-Tarts she bought in 2042.

Behind the PlayStation box is another box, one I never noticed before. It's long and skinny, like a box for enormous spaghetti. It's the brown-green color of dried bay leaves, and the border is covered in a thin line of copper foil. There are no words on it—just a big, copper-foil outline of a triangle on the lid. I open it, and there are a bunch of—I don't know—wooden *Y*s inside? Only they're really long and kind of flexible? So maybe they're not made of wood after all? Who knows? I dump them out on the rug and count them: 44.

My God. The dowsing rods were real. The quote-unquote "Druids" and their pyramid scheme were real. They were realer than the Kleenex I smell when I picture the number *4*. Realer than the Grandma who lives in my glasses. Realer than the stars on Ruby's ceiling. Realer than my relationship with Ezra.

I pull up my text again.

I hit Send.

# CHAPTER 27

Ezra doesn't respond until the next morning.

He texts back one word: "Maybe."

But his maybe must really mean *definitely*, because I don't hear from him for the rest of the day. Or the next day. Or the day after that. Which is fine. Because he doesn't hear from me either.

I ask Grandma—I mean, my real Grandma; my *Grandma*-Grandma—if I should feel bad. Because the thing is, I *don't* feel bad. The thing is, I mainly feel relieved. But Grandma just looks out the window and drums her fingers on the armrest of her new wheelchair and says, "I want to go home."

Mom walks in, sipping a cup of coffee. "You *are* home," she says.

Grandma smacks the armrest. "I want to go *home.*"

"This *is* your home—for the time being, at least. Now, look. Listen. Imagine it's a vacation. Or even a resort! Think of it this way: as long as you're here at The Harbor, you don't have to cook; you don't have to clean. All you have to do is relax and let the nice nurses pamper you and bring you all your meals like you're some kind of queen and help you recover from your surgery—"

"This place is a hellhole."

"It's not a hellhole, Grandma—"

Mom throws up her hands. "Can everyone please stop saying 'hellhole'?"

"Hey," I say. "Check this out." I point to the terracotta frog we brought over from the deck and filled with a new, lush, jungly potted ivy. "And this." I point to the rodeo trophy and ribbons we arranged on her dresser. "And *this*." I point to the frog-shaped bird feeder we bought, filled with sunflower seeds, and suction-cupped to the outside of her window.

Grandma sniffs. "All the birds are dead."

Mom takes off her glasses and squeezes the bridge of her nose.

"We killed them," Grandma says. "That's right. We killed the birds. All of them. And the lightning bugs. Louisa, have you ever even *seen* a lightning bug?"

I haven't, but telling Grandma that seems like a bad idea, so I say, "I've seen the world through their eyes before. It's cool! I used my glasses for it. Do you want to try it?"

*"I used my glasses for it. I used my glasses for it.* Pffft." She shakes her head. "You don't even know what you're talking about, little girl."

Mom clears her throat. She asks Grandma, "Hey, have you seen the nurse lately? Have you taken your—"

"When I was a kid in the '90s, I harassed my parents into taking reusable bags to the Market Basket, and I tried to get them to put a brick in the toilet tank, and I looked up recycling locations in the Yellow Pages without ever actually recycling anything, and I read the *Dawn Saves the Planet* Baby-Sitters Club book, and I called numbers I saw in magazines to get pamphlets about spotted owls and harp seals and polar bears mailed to me, and I paid 30 bucks for a T-shirt with a panda on it because part of the cost went to 'help' the World Wildlife Foundation"—she makes air-quotes around *help*—"and it was all for nothing, y'all. Nothing."

"Come on," I say, "don't be like that. It—"

"And after I grew up and moved from Texas to Florida, I still used reusable shopping bags, and I recycled like a good and nice person, and I composted my fruit and vegetable scraps, and I kept a sad, little, virtuous garden, and every year, that garden never gave me more than a cup of green beans and a single squash.

"Meanwhile, I don't think I've seen a lightning bug in 40 years, and my granddaughter hasn't seen a lightning bug *at all*. And to think I used to run around barefoot on the Fourth of July and catch them in old jelly jars with holes poked in the lids while my dad grilled burgers that were 100% beef and 0% mealworm.

"And we didn't have so many hurricanes that we ran out of people names for them every year and had to start calling them Greek letters. And we didn't have the opposite problems with disease mutations, where we ran out of Greek letters and had to start talking about the Andrea Variant, the Benjamin Variant ... Now the polar bears are dead, and the birds are dead, and the corals are dead, and the Gulf Stream is dead, and my faith in humanity is even more dead than all that.

"And half of the world is flooded, and the other half's on fire, and we even lit *the ocean* on fire a few times—are you old enough to remember that? how old are you, anyway?—and the only reason we haven't flooded or burned Mars yet is that we're still on the way there, for *some* stupid reason. So, what I'm saying is, it's a really good thing I thought about putting a brick in the toilet that one time in 1992. Because it really made a difference, y'all. My God. Just let me rest. I mean it. Let me rest and forget about how sorry I am for five dang minutes."

She closes her eyes. I lay my hand on her arm. "You don't have to be sorry," I say. "You've got years and years ahead of you, and you've already left me with a ton of happy memories."

"I've left my granddaughter with a planet that's a hellhole."

"Again!" Mom says. "'Hellhole'!"

"I left my granddaughter with a world where she'll have to live in a bunker somewhere—eating dehydrated carrots, filtering her pee for drinking water, and poking bandits with sticks."

"Don't be ridiculous," I say. "I'll rehydrate the carrots first." Nobody laughs. I clear my throat. "You've left me with ... with *wisdom*. In fact, listen to this: I need some of your wisdom right now."

Grandma clicks her tongue.

"I'm serious!" I say. "Look. Listen. I broke up with Ezra."

She squints at the birdfeeder where no birds are perched—where, now that I think about it, I have *never* seen a bird perched—and chews on the inside of her left cheek. "Ezra."

"Yeah," I say. "Ezra. You know: my boyfriend. The poseur."

"Are you old enough to have a boyfriend?"

"I'm 14."

"*Fourteen!* And you mean to tell me that they let you work here when you're *14?*"

It sure would be a bad time to have a tic right now. Sure would be bad for my hand to fly off of Grandma's arm and accidentally smack her in the nose and get her blood all over her fancy, motorized wheelchair and these white, lace curtains and this Reba McEntire T-shirt we turned into a throw pillow and set in her lap like some docile pet. I grip her arm a little harder but, hopefully, not too hard. *100 ... 99 ...*

"I don't work here, Grandma. It's me. Louisa." *98 ... 97 ...*

"I guess that's something else we messed up, huh? Kids working at an old folks' home when they're 14 years old. Fourteen-year-old kids ought to be in school, not working at a place like this."

*91 ...* "Well, it's Saturday. And anyway, I—"

"I remember back when COVID came the first time, and nobody wanted to come to work, and there were all these signs trying to get 14- and 15-year-olds to come work at Taco Bell or whatever, and I was like—"

"Grandma. *Grandma.*" *85 ... 84 ...* "It's me."

"Stop shaking me."

"I'm not shaking you." Except I *am* shaking her. I let go of her arm. My fingernails have left indentations in her skin, like tiny crescent moons. I rub them with my palm to make them go away—to erase them. *83 ... 82 ...* "Do you know who I am?" I fold my arms; I squeeze myself tight. "You do, don't you? Don't you?"

And while Mom sing-songs, "Oh, of *course*, she does; I'm sure she does," in a voice that means she isn't even slightly sure, my arms slip out of my control—like a dog pulling its leash from your hand and running, barking, into traffic—and my fingertips graze the tip of Grandma's nose.

"Help!" Grandma yells. "Help! Nurse! Help!" And it takes me a second to realize she's not calling for a nurse to help *me*. She's calling for a nurse to protect her *from* me.

Somebody grabs the back of my collar and pulls me a few steps back. I spin around and almost punch them in the liver before I realize it's not some bad guy; it's a nurse, and oh wait, it's not a nurse, it's my mom, and she's pulling me into a little, wooden chair with a red-and-white checkered cushion, and she's saying, "Okaaaay. Let's slooow down for a sec. Let's all just slooow down."

I expect to see blood on my hand, on Grandma's face, on *something*, but there isn't any. There's not even a scratch on her nose—at least, not as far as *I* can tell. But she keeps on yelling for help until Mom pats her hand and says *hush* over and over again. *Hush now. Husssh.* Out the window, a squirrel scampers onto the birdfeeder, but it's the squirrel-proof, cage-looking kind, so the squirrel just bites and claws, for nothing. *Hush now.*

"I'm sorry," I tell Grandma. "It was an accident."

She balls up the corner of the Reba pillow in her fist.

"It's me," I say. "It's Louisa. Do you remember who I am?"

Grandma stares at my charm bracelet. She stares at my face. Then her eyebrows go up like *ah!*, and then she smiles and says, "I do now."

For a second, no one says anything. And then I start shoveling words into the pit of silence, to fill it: "Ezra got me this bracelet. You remember him, don't you? Ezra? My boyfriend? At least, he *was* my boyfriend. I don't know *what* he is now. I should probably stop wearing this since we're not, like, *together* anymore, but I don't know: I still kind of like it. But I also kind of *don't*. Because it reminds me that I should feel bad that we're broken up—I mean, that we're *sort of* broken up—but I don't actually feel that bad about it. Like, shouldn't I be looking through the pictures of his Shaman drawings and being like, 'Oh, I remember when he gave the Shaman that hat with antlers on it. We were so much happier then,' instead of— you know—*not* doing that? But I've been practicing for my hapkido test and rereading the issues of *Mera* where she travels to Jupiter's moons and doing other normal stuff like that, and I don't know, I've just been living, if that makes sense, and *does* that make sense?"

Grandma doesn't answer. She steers her chair toward the terracotta frog in the corner—like *whirrr*—and she runs her fingers over the ivy. She does it so gently that you'd think each leaf was covered in a crackled film of actual gold. "I don't like frogs," she says. "I never liked frogs."

# CHAPTER 28

The trampoline in Ruby's yard still feels warm even though the sun set a while ago. Lying back on it feels like lying on the hood of a car you just turned off.

"The fake stars are better," I tell her.

"What?"

"The fake stars. The ones on your ceiling. They're better."

"Well, you can't judge the night sky based on *this*." She sits up and waves her hand at the sky, which looks like a giant sheet of gray construction paper. "There's too much light pollution. You've got to get out in the Everglades or something to really appreciate it." She picks a blade of grass or a clump of dirt—or maybe some imaginary something— off of the bottom of her flip flop and throws it into the not-quite-darkness of the yard. "We should go sometime."

"To the *Everglades*?"

"Yeah. I mean, if you—"

"I'd love to go."

She scratches her big toe. "It's not like we've got a trip planned or anything, but my parents have been talking about maybe going there in the spring, and if—"

"I'd love to go."

She looks at me like *really?*

I look at her like *really.*

I sit up, too. "Hey, did I ever tell you about the time my grandma said I should take somebody to the Everglades to, like, *disappear* them if they gave me a hard time?"

Ruby laughs. "What? No! You did *not* mention that."

"She was 99% joking—or, I guess *you* would say she was 99.999% joking—but I'm pretty sure she was 0.001% not joking."

"Oh my God, *please* don't kill me in the Everglades."

"I won't kill you in the—"

"Pinky-swear." She holds up her pinky finger. "Pinky-swear that you won't kill me in the Everglades."

We laugh. I grab her pinky finger with mine. She grabs mine back. We stop laughing. A stare at her earring: a tiny, pale-pink crystal dangling from her left earlobe. She pulls her pinky away, sits on her hands, and stares at the lotus-flower flag that's rippling in the back-porch light.

"How's your grandma doing anyway?" she asks.

"She's ..." I sigh. "She's fine, I guess. I mean, her *leg* is fine. And she hasn't wrecked any more cars or started any more fires. And everyone at The Harbor is really nice. Like, they're really and truly nice. And sometimes Grandma seems to like it well enough there. But sometimes she whines about wanting to go home, which I guess I can understand because there are some residents who are *really*, well, *you* know. Like, there's this container garden in the lobby, with these fancy red-and-blue lights hung over the plants, right? And the other day, I saw this old guy picking peapods off the dwarf pea plants and putting them in his hoodie pockets, and the whole time he was muttering, 'They rally 'round the family with a pocket full of shells. They rally 'round the family with a pocket full of shells.'[ii] I mean, that's crazy, right? Like, what does it even *mean*?" I pull my knees up to my chest and hug them. "And, also, sometimes Grandma doesn't remember who I am."

"Oh, wow, I'm really sorry. That sounds hard. That's ... I'm just really sorry."

"Yeah, it's ..." I force myself to laugh. "It's something else all right."

Ruby hugs her knees the way I am. We're a matched set now. She's like, "Sometimes when my problems seem bigger than I can handle, I remind myself that, in the grand scheme of things, they're not so big after all. In a thousand years, humans probably won't exist anymore. In a million years, Neil Armstrong's footprints will fade from the surface of the Moon. In five million years, the pyramids will erode. In five billion years, the sun will die. In a hundred billion years, every star like it will die, too. In 30 thousand trillion trillion years, black holes will absorb all matter in the universe. In 10 trillion trillion trillion trillion trillion trillion—"

"OK," I laugh. "I get it."

"—trillion trillion years, the last black hole will evaporate, and space-time will cease to exist. So, there. Isn't that calming to think about?"

"No."

"No?"

"No! It's *terrifying*."

"But I was trying to make you feel *better*! Here. Here, I know. This'll make you feel better. Stand up. Stand *up*. I'll teach you how to do jump-style kicks, only we'll do it on the trampoline, and I'll double-bounce you, so you'll get *really* high."

"But I thought you weren't allowed to teach me new stuff," I say, getting up. "I thought you could only help me review old stuff. I thought it was a rule."

"Yeah, well." She shrugs and walks to the edge of the trampoline. "Start jumping," she tells me. "Get a good rhythm going. You know, when I was going up for my yellow belt, I never wanted to practice for it. Part of it was that I had this *other* test to study for. It was this earth-science test about strata, or rock layers. But the other part of it was that I was just being lazy. So, my parents did a tarot reading to inspire me to practice."

"Really?" I say, jumping. "That's so cool!"

"Yeah. And the first card they drew was the six of wands, which shows some guy wearing a victory wreath and riding a horse in front of a crowd that's cheering him on, like he just came home from a successful battle or something. It's all about winning and triumph and stuff like that."

"So, you got off your butt and practiced?"

"Of course not. I kept reading about rocks. But I *thought* about getting off my butt and practicing. And that's better than nothing."

"But you passed your test, right?"

"Oh, yeah. Yeah, totally."

"Because you practiced later."

A grin spreads across her face.

I gasp. "You didn't practice! *You!* You, of all people! That seems so—I don't know—so unlike you, somehow."

"I know, I know. I *should* have practiced. I was just distracted by, like, that test. And there was this whole other test I had in social studies on the same day. And I had this application I had to fill out for a summer camp. Because for *that* I had to write this whole two-page essay, right? Because the camp was run by NASA—"

"You just didn't want to do it."

"I just didn't want to do it."

We laugh.

"*You're* going to practice, though," she tells me. "I'm going to make you practice. Here. I'm going to double-bounce you, and you're going to do jump-style kick five, only you'll do it over my head."

"*What?*"

"Yeah, just watch." She comes closer to me and jumps *right* before my feet hit the trampoline. The trampoline snaps back with such force that it sends me twice as high as usual. I can see the frisbee stuck on her roof. I can see the collapsing jack-o-lantern that's still on her neighbor's porch, on the other side of the fence. "Kick!" she yells. So, I do. My foot flies over her head with tons of room to spare.

Ruby applauds. Then she grabs both of my hands, and we jump together. Her bangs and her earrings look weightless every time she descends. I'm about to tell her she looks like an honest-to-goodness astronaut in an honest-to-goodness spaceship, but she says, really fast, "I-want-to-show-you-something-else-jump-style-OK?"

"Um, OK?"

"A jump-style kick."

"Which one?"

She stares at me.

"Which one?" I say again. "Which kick?"

Her eyes get wide. It's the face you make when you push back the shower curtain and see a spider by the drain. "No, not—Not a jump-style *kick*. A jump-style *kiss*. But it's fine. It's fine; we don't have to—"

"OK."

"OK, what?"

"OK, show me. Show me a jump-style kiss."

# CHAPTER 29

"Explain this to me again," Mom says, putting a spoonful of Crick-or-Treat in her mouth. "*How* did you bust your lip?"

"It's not busted. It's just ... sore."

She snorts. "Sore enough for you to hold your pint of Crick-or-Treat against it for five minutes. Like, bruh, it's going to melt. In fact ... it *is*. It's melting already. If you're just going to use it to ice your lip, then put it back in the freezer and get an icepack instead. If you're going to eat it, then *eat* it."

"I'll eat it. OK?"

"It's seasonal. It's limited edition."

"I said, *I'll eat it.*"

She hands me a spoon. "Then eat."

We're sitting in front of the fridge, on the kitchen floor, which has never been this shiny before. No dirt. No crumbs. No grease spatters.

No peanut shells. No leathery potato peels. No dried-out marshmallows. No cheesy gobs of splat.

The fridge isn't covered with magnets and menus anymore. It's a big, gleaming, silver rectangle. The rooster-print dishtowel is gone from the oven door. Mom replaced it with a plain, white one that's as bright as my hapkido uniform. The whole room smells like lemons, only it's—I don't know—aggressive? It's aggressively lemony. It's even cleaner in here than when Ruby came over. Only this time, I can't stand it.

I dribble some of my melted ice cream on the floor. There. That's better.

Mom clicks her tongue. "Come on, Louisa. Really?"

"It was an accident," I lie.

Mom rolls her eyes. "I still don't understand how you got hurt. You say this happened when you were practicing for your test with Ruby, but if *you* were kicking at *her*, shouldn't *she* be the one with the busted lip? Paint me a picture. Make me understand."

But even if I told her this happened from a kiss, she wouldn't understand. Not really. She'd never understand that some kisses feel like kick 17, the kneeling back kick. It's a kick you do behind you. It's easy to miss your target because you have to touch the ground—like downward dog in yoga—and look at the bad guy upside down while not falling on your head. With kisses like that, everything feels awkward, and all the blood is rushing to your head, and you can hardly tell where your lips happen to land or what they do when they get there.

Other kisses feel like kick ten, the front thrust heel kick. It's the kick you think of when you imagine a firefighter kicking in a door. No worrying, no weird balancing acts. Just *blam*, and the door flies open, and all the heat behind the door comes roaring out. And if you get hurt, it's still worth it.

So, I say, "It's a hapkido thing. You wouldn't understand."

For a while, we eat our ice cream in silence. Then Mom says, "I like this girl, you know."

"What girl?" I say, like I don't already know.

"Ruby. She's smart. And nice. And nice *to you*."

I use my spoon to dig a cricket out of the carton and crunch down on it. "Did Grandma really never like frogs?" I ask. "Was that true, what she said? Or did she forget she liked them? Or what?"

Mom sighs. "I don't know. I've been asking myself the same thing. Because I'm pretty sure I gave her that frog planter for Mother's Day, when I was in high school, and I'm starting to wonder if that was the first frog thing she ever had. If it *was*, then maybe she acted appreciative, just to be polite. 'Oh, I *love* it! Frogs are so quirky! I just *adore* them.' You know, like *that*. Maybe she was so convincing that I thought she really liked frogs, and I got her more frogs in the future. And then maybe other people saw *those* frogs, and *they* got her frogs, too. And maybe, next thing your Grandma knew, she was an accidental frog collector. Or—OK, seriously, I can't stand it anymore." She gets the dishtowel off the oven door and wipes the ice cream off of the floor. "Or, maybe she's always liked frogs, and she misremembers it," she says, rinsing the dishtowel at the sink. "I just can't tell anymore. I mean, I honestly just can't tell. But, anyway, don't change the subject. What's going on between you and Ruby? Have you asked her out yet? Because you should ask her out."

"Oh my God, Mom, you're worse than Grandma."

"Well, *have* you?"

"No." I put the lid back on my ice cream. "She asked me out, though."

"She *did*? Why didn't you *tell* me?"

"Because—*Ow!*"

Mom snaps the dishtowel at me. "Where are you going? What are you going to wear? What is *she* going to wear? Oh! You two should coordinate your outfits. You should wear your black dress with the fringe and the spangly bits. Black will coordinate with anything she decides to wear. Now, what about flowers?"

"This."

"She strikes me as a daisy kind of person. We can order a bouquet of them. Or one of those deals with a stuffed bear. You know what I mean."

"*This* is why I didn't tell you."

She sends an ad to my lenses: a hippo hugging a vase of daisies with a purple ribbon wrapped around it.

"Oh!" she says. "For $10 more, it comes with a little hat."

I drop my spoon in the sink, put the ice cream back in the freezer, and get out an icepack. "I'm taking your advice," I say. "I'm going to go ice my lip. It's hurting again." I mean, it *isn't*—not much, anyway—but maybe if I go ice it in my room, she'll leave me alone.

Now a stuffed Dalmatian fills my lenses. All of its spots are heart-shaped. It's holding a red rose between its front paws.

I walk to my room.

"Look!" Mom calls after me. "This one's customizable!" She sends me another picture of the Dalmatian, only this time, it's wearing a collar with a heart-shaped tag that says, "NAME."

I slam my door behind me. I clear my lenses, flop down on my bed, and stare at the beige splotch on the ceiling. I text Grandma to let her know that Ruby asked me out, but she doesn't text back, and I have no way of knowing whether that's because she's eating, she's asleep, she's putting together a puzzle, she's doing the watermelon crawl with the other residents, she forgot to charge her phone, she forgot *how* to charge her phone, or she forgot who I am. So, I tell quote-unquote "Grandma" instead.

I tell "Grandma" that we're going to an aquarium together. I tell her I've never been to a real aquarium before, but Ruby had me take the virtual tour of this one, and it looks magical. There's a restaurant there, too, and that's where we'll have lunch, but they serve sushi there, and isn't that weird? Eating dead fish in front of live fish?

"Grandma" agrees. It's definitely weird. And believe her: she knows weird when she sees it. She's seen Crystal Pepsi. She's seen layered socks. She's seen TV shows about cars that solve crimes. Yeah. She's seen weird, all right.

I tell "Grandma" about my belt test, and how it's making me nervous, and how every time I try to run through what it'll be on it, I forget at least one thing—sometimes more. I tell her kick two—the diagonal snapping toe kick—is especially hard because you have to do this leany thing with your head, and I'm always doing it the wrong way or not at all.

"Grandma" tells me to show her this kick two. And even though I know she can't see me—even though I know there's no actual Grandma there *to* see me—I get up and do it. And she says it looks phenomenal. She says I look like one of the sunflowers that used to grow in front of her house. And even though I don't know what exactly that's supposed to mean, it *does* make me feel better.

I sigh and sit back down on the bed. I glance around the room. The treadmill's still here, but it has *my* clothes hanging on it now. The Lorrie Morgan poster is down, and my cat clock is up. The only things on the desk are my figurines, my Mera mug full of number-two pencils, and some worksheets that are due Monday and that I really should have finished already.

The Revolutionary War isn't being fought on the other side of my wall anymore. Sheriffs aren't shooting train robbers. The police aren't shooting zombies. The only sound is the ticking of the clock as the cat's eyes and tail move back and forth. I finally have all the quiet I've been craving since I moved here.

*"OK, Grandma: I want to go home."*

She looks confused. "But, you *are* home, aren't you?"

"Yes. And no. Mainly no."

"I know it's hard, but you can't go back to where you were. Hurricane Louisa was a Category 5 storm, with windspeeds upward of 170 miles per hour and a catastrophic 17-foot storm surge—"

"Are you just reading the news?" I mumble.

"—and it caused $180 billion in damage. You're one of the thousands of Floridians the storm displaced."

"OK, you are definitely reading the news right now. That's not what I'm talking about, Grandma, all right? It's hard to explain."

"Then what *are* you talking about? Where is home?"

I snort. "More like '*When* is home?'" I remember the icepack and hold it against my lip. I get under the covers. I lie on my back; I roll onto my side; I hug three pillows. I can't get comfortable, no matter what I do. So, I throw the covers back, toss the icepack on the floor, lock myself in the bathroom, and turn the shower on full blast. I sit on the rug and wait for the room to fill with steam. My glasses fog up. I try to imagine some blacksmith—beard, black apron, leather gloves—clanging a piece of metal with a hammer. I imagine the hissing when he plunges the metal into a barrel of cold water. I try to imagine this feeling—this sadness, this loneliness, this whatever it is—hardening into a more useful emotion, like contentment. Or peace.

It doesn't work.

*"OK, Grandma: Tell me about the house you lived in when you were growing up."*

"When I was growing up, we lived in a white house with a fence in front, and all these sunflowers. We kept this 60- or 70-gallon fish tank in the bathroom. There was Spongebob's pineapple house in it, and this scuba diver who went up and down. And we had these rainbow fish."

I lie down on the rug even though it's damp—even though everything in this bathroom is always damp. I stare at the little springy thing that sticks out from the baseboard and keeps the door from slamming into the wall when you open it too hard.

"There was this little table where your great-grandma would keep her makeup and lotion in these little drawers. And sometimes your great-grandma would make me mad because she made me clean my room. So, I'd take a hate shower. I'd sit on this lavender rug we had in the bathroom, and I'd let the shower run, and I'd watch the whole bathroom turn into a steam room."

With my finger, I trace my own invisible sigil on the rug, like the one Ruby has on her short stick. I draw an *M*. Then, right below it, I draw a *W*. It looks like two mountains reflected in a lake. I add an *H* and an *L* that, together, look like a hammock between two trees. And I make a *C* into a crescent moon.

*W L C M H*

*WELCOME HOME*

"And I wouldn't even feel mad anymore. I'd feel calm. But I'd also feel ready to fight."

I smile because the rug still smells like a dish sponge.

# CHAPTER 30

"So. Tube worms."

I laugh. "Weird first-official-date topic—even if that date is at an aquarium—but OK."

"They get their nutrients from hydrothermal vents in the ocean," Ruby says, "but they can grow to be seven feet long. And they live so deep underwater that we didn't even discover them until, like, *years* after we landed on the moon."

"Well, *I* was going to say that this Xebel exhibit is cool, but sure, tube worms work, too."

We wander from Xebel—with its eels winding around Mera's castle and its crabs clinging to her chariot—to a see-through column full of see-through jellyfish that has nothing to do with Mera or any other comic. The column must have a special light in it, because the jellyfish are glowing lime green as they bop along. Even Ruby looks green when she stands on the other side of the column. So does her white headband and the temporary tattoo of a dove on her neck.

She walks around to my side. "Hey, maybe your grandma would like to come here sometime. You can still, like, check her out for day trips, right? She's not in prison."

"Yeah, she'd probably like it. I mean, how could anyone *not* like this place?" I sweep my arm in front of me, like *look at all this stuff!*

We drift over the carpet that looks like blue and green ripples to a coral reef exhibit taking up an entire wall. My glasses tell me this is what the reef would have looked like at the turn of the century. It's so huge. And colorful. Like a multi-flavor pack of popsicles.

"I can't believe you love fish as much as you do, and you've never been to a real aquarium before," Ruby says.

"Well, I can't believe you love space as much as you do, and you've never been to—I don't know—an observatory before."

Ruby grins. "Actually, I *have* been to an observatory."

"Why does that not surprise me?"

"I've heard—Wait. Your tag's sticking up." She reaches behind my neck and pushes my shirt tag back down. My breath catches in my throat. I hope she doesn't notice. "I've heard there are parts of space that we know more about than we do the deepest parts of the ocean. Isn't that wild?"

"That can't be true. Is that true?"

"I think it's true."

I watch a clownfish—which I can identify without help, Glazier, thank you very much—glide through the swaying, peach tentacles of a sea anemone. A yellow fish—as bright as the filling in Mom's lemon meringue pie—flits by. My glasses tell me it's a yellow tang.

"The day we moved Grandma into The Harbor, she told me she was sorry for letting the corals die, as if she did it personally. Like, seriously: she felt *really* bad about it. And after that is when she forgot who I was. So maybe I *shouldn't* bring her here? Maybe it would set her off? Like, I don't know."

Ruby gets a faraway look, like she's looking through the coral reef exhibit instead of into it. "What if ... what if *we* led an activity at The

Harbor, for your Grandma and the other residents? Some of us from the dojang, I mean. Do you think we could teach them some simple techniques? Escaping from some wrist grabs, doing some joint locks—that kind of thing? Master Avery would lead it. And we could help. After all, you're a yellow belt now." She nudges me. "Everybody hear that? She's a *yellow belt.*"

I blush, even though there's only one other person in the room, and he's not paying any attention to us. "Oh my God," I say, laughing, "stop."

"OK, OK. But that *does* mean you've mastered how to escape from an elbow grab—to name just *one* thing—so you can absolutely help them with *that.* And I can help them with higher-belt things, like blocking punches."

"And getting out of rear-collar grabs. And rear-shoulder grabs. And—hey!—Charlotte could show them techniques from a chair," I say. I clap my hands. "You're a genius, Ruby. This is a great idea. Truly."

"Hey, it's your idea, too."

We walk back to the moon jellies and watch them drift through the green water. It's like they're floating through space.

"You know what I like most about hapkido?" Ruby says. "You can't fake it. What I mean is, when you test for a new belt, you either do the techniques properly, or you don't. That's it. You can't cheat your way through it. If you try to throw someone, either they fall or they don't. If you do a joint lock on them, either it's painful or it's not. It's an honest art. It's genuine." She wraps her arm around mine. "I guess I just really like things that are genuine."

# CHAPTER 31

I think we're missing a corner piece, but Ruby swears we're not.

And Grandma's like, "She's right, Louisa. We just took the shrink wrap off of the box. We couldn't have lost a piece already. It didn't fall in your yellow belt, did it?"

I run my hand along the inside of my belt even though it's impossible for a puzzle piece to get wedged in there. Then I swirl the pieces around on Grandma's table, looking for one with two straight sides. "Y'all, it's not here, I promise."

"Did you know they have a siren at the factory where they make these puzzles, and anytime someone sees a random puzzle piece lying on the floor, they set it off, and everyone stops what they're doing to figure out where it came from?" Ruby says. "True story."

"Ah-ha!" Grandma holds up the missing piece. "I was sitting on it."

Ruby slaps my leg with one end of her brown belt. "*Told* you it was here."

We barely have time to fit the corner piece into the snowy sky above a barn before it's time to leave. We'd lost track of the time.

I roll Grandma toward her door. Ruby follows us. We pass the frog-themed Christmas tree on her nightstand, the new ten-gallon tank with four frogs darting around it, and the jigsaw puzzles we've mounted on the walls like art. Pretty soon the barn will be up there, too. When I close the door behind us, the wreath on it jingles. It has green bells on it, shaped like little frog faces. She seems to like frogs again. Or maybe she always did. Or maybe she never did, and she's just remembered how to fake it.

Everyone's door has *something* on it: a watercolor snowman; a Bible verse; a Rage Against the Machine poster; *Far Side* comic strips tacked to a bulletin board; a whiteboard that says, "With my grandbabies! Back January 2." And all the way down the hall, it's *Hey, Sarah! Where you headed, Sarah? How you been, Sarah? Ready for Christmas, Sarah?*

And Grandma's like, *Hey, Jessica! Going to hapkido. You want to come, too? Well, come on, then, get a move on! Been doing all right, Heather, and yourself? All right, all right, happy to hear it. Oh, Bella's got me all fixed up. Got a tree and ornaments and lights and everything.*

As we're leaving The Harbor, one woman knitting in the foyer puts down her needles, smiles at the three of us, and says, "Got your granddaughters with you today, huh, Sarah?"

And I can tell that Grandma doesn't know quite how to answer this question. She doesn't look the woman in the face—instead, she looks at the basket of yarn at her feet—and she giggles even though nothing's funny. "Oh, Ruby and Louisa are my two best girls. The best." Which is a brilliant answer, really, because it's not an answer at all.

Maybe right now she knows I'm her granddaughter, and Ruby's my girlfriend. Maybe she thinks we're both granddaughters to her. Maybe she thinks we both work for The Harbor. Maybe she thinks we're hapkido instructors—or karate instructors. Maybe she thinks we're Girl Scouts volunteering here to earn a very obscure and very violent merit badge.

On the way to the food court, I try to imagine what it's like to be her—in this place, at this moment—and any of those explanations would make sense. We're two teenagers in martial arts uniforms, spending time with her and taking her to an activity. I tell myself the important thing is that we're "her two best girls." I tell myself the other labels don't matter. And today I believe it. Almost.

My thoughts are interrupted when Ruby grabs my hand. For the first time, I see panic in her eyes. "It's going to be good, right?" she asks.

"Ruby Fernández, are you *nervous*?"

She rubs my knuckle with her thumb. "Maybe."

Grandma says over her shoulder, "Girl, you've got nothing to worry about. I've got a bunch of my friends coming, and if they don't act right, I give you permission to beat the ever-living daylights out of them."

Ruby's like, "Thank you?"

I swing Ruby's arm back and forth. "But you won't need to beat anybody up because everybody's going to love it."

We turn the corner at the pretzel place. Master Avery is already there, talking to the activity director, who is wearing a sweatband with a Japanese flag on it. Eh. Close enough. Charlotte is writing something on a clipboard. Six residents are already waiting for the program to start. One of them is finishing a pretzel and brushing salt off his shirt. Another one sees Grandma and waves.

Grandma waves back. And something about it—the way she waggles her fingers, the way she holds her hand high over her head, *something*—reminds me of when we told her goodbye after Thanksgiving last year. I remember her red dress with the white trim that looked like cake icing that a baker piped on. I remember her shiny, black shoes with the heels and the ankle straps. And she'll never stand in those shoes and wave at us again, will she? I'll never watch her get smaller and smaller out of the back window of a car while we drive away, will I? We'll never spill her gravy. We'll never spill another tray full of splat.

I tell myself I won't cry in a food court. I won't, I won't. It's too pathetic.

Right now, Grandma is smiling, and I concentrate on that. Right now, she's talking to this guy about a *Friends*-themed lunch they're all having at The Harbor next week. Right now, I'm one of her best girls. I don't know exactly what that means. And I don't exactly *care* what it means. All I care is that it feels good to hear it.

I close my eyes. I try to trap this moment in my brain before the memory dissolves like the confectioner's sugar in one of Mom's glazes. I listen closely as Grandma says, "Of course Phoebe was my favorite. Phoebe was everybody's favorite." I focus on the buttery smell of the pretzel place; the random accordion music that's drifting over from somewhere; the weight of my glasses on my nose as quote-unquote "Grandma" pops up to say, 'I heard a song like that at the rodeo once!' (I dismiss her); the way Ruby's turquoise ring feels smooth against my fingers; the rubber-band feeling that's growing in my arms.

I open my eyes. I wrap Ruby in a side hug to stop the tic from coming on.

I wonder if Grandma's shoes with the ankle straps had silver buckles or gold ones. Were the buttons on the dress white or black? Did the dress have buttons at all? Maybe it had a zipper. It bothers me that I can't remember these things. They're so basic—so obvious. Why can't I remember?

Ruby twists the turquoise ring around and around her finger. "What if Master Avery says it's my turn to demonstrate something, but I just, like, *stand* there?" she whispers to me. "What if I forget what I'm supposed to do?"

When Ezra kissed me—before we left town—what color was the paint on his T-shirt? I'm pretty sure it was blue, but maybe it was purple. Or maybe the paint wasn't on his T-shirt at all. Maybe it was on his pants.

Will I remember this hug with Ruby a year from now? What about 10 years? What about 50? Will I remember her turquoise ring when I'm Grandma's age? Will I remember her NASA backpack? Will I remember her spice-racky smell?

I squeeze Ruby tighter. "Just have fun, and do the best you can," I say. "There are worse things in life than forgetting."

# ABOUT THE AUTHOR

Photo by Dave Ryan

A West Virginia native, Stacey Elza earned her B.A. in English from McNeese State University in Lake Charles, La., and her M.F.A. in creative writing from West Virginia University in Morgantown, W.Va. Her writing has appeared in *The Lion and the Unicorn, Iron Horse Literary Review*, the Unitarian Universalist WorshipWeb Library, and *ADDitude Magazine*. She has a second-degree black belt in hapkido—a Korean martial art—which she earned at the American Judo-Hapkido Institute. She lives in Morgantown with her husband, two daughters, and two cats.

# LYRICS REFERENCED

[i] David Bowie. "Life on Mars," track 6 on *Hunky Dory*, RCA Records, 1971.

[ii] Rage Against the Machine. "Bulls on Parade," track 2 on *Evil Empire*, Epic Records, 1996.

www.ingramcontent.com/pod-product-compliance
Lightning Source LLC
Chambersburg PA
CBHW060852210726
48293CB00006B/1769